Her cane.

She stared at the snazzy pink length of metal—she'd gone for the bright, cheerful color, hoping to jazz up the fact of her disability—and the fizz evaporated from her stomach. The smile died on her lips. She knew full well Sean Granger hadn't spotted her cane in her car or he never would have taken the time to talk with her. This she knew from personal experience.

"Well, duty calls." Sean pushed away and offered her a dashing grin, making time stand still. She sat captivated by the wholesome goodness of the man as he tipped his hat to her. "I'll see you around, Eloise Tipple."

"Bbb—" The closest thing she could manage to goodbye, but he didn't seem to notice her jumbled attempt at speech. He loped away with a relaxed, confident stride and hopped into his truck.

It wasn't until Eloise had pulled onto the street heading away from town that it struck her. Sean Granger had remembered her name.

Books by Jillian Hart

Love Inspired

*A Soldier for Christmas
*Precious Blessings
*Every Kind of Heaven
*Everyday Blessings
*A McKaslin Homecoming
A Holiday to Remember
*Her Wedding Wish
*Her Perfect Man
Homefront Holiday
*A Soldier for Keeps
*Blind-Date Bride
†The Soldier's Holiday Vow
†The Rancher's Promise
Klondike Hero
†His Holiday Bride
†His Country Girl
†Wyoming Sweethearts

Love Inspired Historical

*Homespun Bride
*High Country Bride
In a Mother's Arms
  "Finally a Family"
**Gingham Bride
**Patchwork Bride
**Calico Bride

*The McKaslin Clan
†The Granger Family Ranch
**Buttons & Bobbins

JILLIAN HART

grew up on her family's homestead, where she helped raise cattle, rode horses and scribbled stories in her spare time. After earning her English degree from Whitman College, she worked in travel and advertising before selling her first novel. When Jillian isn't working on her next story, she can be found puttering in her rose garden, curled up with a good book or spending quiet evenings at home with her family.

Wyoming Sweethearts

Jillian Hart

Love Inspired

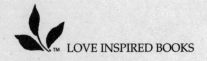

LOVE INSPIRED BOOKS

ISBN-13: 978-0-373-87685-3

WYOMING SWEETHEARTS

Copyright © 2011 by Jill Strickler

www.LoveInspiredBooks.com

Printed in U.S.A.

I will sing to the Lord,
because He has dealt bountifully with me.
—*Psalms* 13:6

To Keneta

Chapter One

"Do you know what your problem is, Eloise?"

"I didn't know I had a problem, Gran." Eloise Tipple held the diner's heavy glass door for her frail grandmother and resisted the urge to roll her eyes. Her helpful gran had been doling out a lot of advice over the past three months, ever since Eloise returned home to the small town of Wild Horse, Wyoming. "When I look at my life, I see blue skies. No trouble of any kind."

"Then you aren't looking closely enough, my dear." Edie Tipple padded by, the hem of her sensible summer dress fluttering lightly in the wind. "Your life has been derailed. I intend to fix that."

"It wasn't derailed, Gran. I had a car accident, not a train accident," she quipped. She let the diner's door swoosh shut, adjusted her pink metallic cane and followed the sprightly elderly lady toward a gleaming 1963 Ford Falcon. She hoped humor would derail her grandmother because Eloise knew precisely what track Edie was on. "Are you going to stop by the church before you head home?"

"Don't try and change the subject on me." Gran

hauled open her car door. "It wasn't fair the way you lost your career and your fiancé."

"We had only discussed marriage, he hadn't actually proposed to me."

"That's still a big loss. It cost you so much." Gran rolled down the window, cranking away on the old-fashioned handle. "I have a solution in mind."

"A solution?" Oh, boy. She gave her long blond hair a toss. The car accident had ended her ice-dancing career, a career she had desperately loved, and her heart had been broken by a man who left her for someone else. At twenty-four, a girl didn't want to feel as if the best part of her life was behind her. She didn't want to think there were no more dreams left in store. "You don't mean another blind date?"

"There's nothing blind about it. I know the boy's grandmother. He's the one for you, Eloise. I can feel it in my bones." Gran folded herself elegantly behind the wheel, diminutive in stature but great of spirit. Her silver curls fluttered with the brush of the breeze as she clicked her lap belt.

"I don't want to go on another fix-up." Eloise gently closed the heavy car door with a thud. "The last twelve have been complete disasters. I don't want to be tortured anymore."

"How hard can it be to have a nice dinner with a young man?" Gran recovered her car key from behind the visor and plugged it into the ignition. The engine roared to life with a rumble and a big puff of smoke. "His name is George, and he's an up-and-comer. I have it on good authority that he's a hard worker and very tidy. That's important when you're considering a man as marriage material."

"Sure. I'll make a note of it." Eloise, unable to stop herself, rolled her eyes.

"I saw that, young lady." Gran chuckled. "You don't want to work at the inn for the rest of your days, do you?"

"I don't know. I like my job. I'm trying not to look too far ahead. My future may be an endless line of one blind date after another. Scary. Better to live in the moment." She pushed away from the car door. "Thanks for meeting me for lunch, Gran."

"Then I'll tell Madge to tell George it's a date." Gran put the car into reverse. "Friday night at the diner. Don't frown, dear. Hebrews 11:1. Believe."

"I'll try." At this point, she was a skeptic when it came to happily-ever-afters. She was recovering from a broken heart. Love hadn't turned out well for her. Could she endure one more blind date?

She simply would have to find a way. The hot, late May sun chased her as she circled around to her car, slipped behind the steering wheel and dropped onto the vinyl seat. Hot, hot, hot. Eloise rolled down the window and switched on the air conditioner, which sputtered unenthusiastically. She swiped bangs from her forehead and backed out of the space.

Now faith is the substance of things hoped for, the evidence of things not seen. That was the verse Gran had referenced, and it stayed on her mind as she drove down the dusty, one-horse main street. The precise stretch of sidewalk-lined shops, the march of trees from one end of town to the other, hadn't changed much since she was a child.

Way up ahead on the empty street, a pair of ponies plodded into sight, ridden by two little girls heading toward the drive-in. They were probably getting ice cream. Memories welled up, good ones that made her smile as she motored toward the library.

She caught sight of the grill of the sheriff's Jeep peeking around the lilac bush next to the library sign. Sheriff Ford Sherman had his radar set up and was probably reading a Western paperback to pass the time between the span of cars.

She glanced at her speedometer—twenty-four miles an hour. Safe. She waved at the sheriff who looked up from his book and waved back.

Ice cream. That was an idea. There was nothing like the Steer In's soft ice-cream cones. Her mouth watered, clinching her decision. She had plenty of time left on her lunch hour and the temptation was too great to resist.

She hit her signal, crossed over the dotted yellow line and rolled into the drive-in's lot. The girls on their ponies had ridden up to the window in the drive-thru lane and one of the animals looked a little nervously at the approaching car's grill, so she slipped into a slot and parked beneath the shady awning. A brightly lit and yellowed display menu perched above an aging speaker. She rolled her window down the rest of the way and hot, dry air breezed in, no match for the struggling air conditioner.

"Eloise!" A teenager on roller skates gave an awkward wave and almost dropped her loaded tray. "Hi!"

"Hi, Chloe." She unbuckled so she could lean out the window. Chloe Walters still had the exuberant disposition she'd had as a small child, when Eloise had babysat her. "That's right, school is out for the year. Are you a senior now?"

"Yep. One more year and freedom." Chloe nearly dropped her tray again as she swept forward on choppy strokes of her skates and grabbed the edge of the speaker so she wouldn't crash into the car. "It's so cool you are working at the inn. We went there for dinner for Mom's birthday and it was really fancy."

"It is a nice place to work." The Lord had been looking out for her when she'd landed the job as executive manager at the Lark Song Inn. Good thing she had a business degree to fall back on. "How about you? I didn't know you worked at the drive-in."

"It's new. I really love it. I get all the ice cream I can eat." She grinned, her smile perfect now that her braces were off, and nearly spilled the contents of her tray yet again. "I'd better go deliver this before it melts. Do you know what you want?"

"A small chocolate soft ice-cream cone." The large size was tempting, but she'd never get it eaten before she was back behind the front desk. "Thanks, Chloe."

"I'll get it in just a minute!" The teenager, eager to please, dashed off with a *clump, clump* of her skates.

A big, dark blue pickup rolled to a stop in the space beside her. Tinted windows shielded any glimpse of the driver, but she recognized the look of a ranch truck when she saw it. The haphazard blades of hay caught in the frame of the cab's back window, dust on the mud flaps and the tie-downs marching along the bed were all telltale signs. The heavy duty engine rumbled like a monster as it idled, a testimony to the payload it was capable of hauling.

Chloe, her tray now empty, skated as fast as she could go up to the far side of the pickup. Eloise lost sight of the teenager, but judging by the speed with which she'd crossed the lot, it was someone she knew or wanted to. Remembering what it was like to be a teenager in this town, she smiled. She'd worked part-time in the library after school shelving books and hadn't had the chance to meet too many cute high school boys on the job. A serious downside to being a librarian's assistant.

An electronic jangle caught her attention, and she reached over the gearshift to dig through the outside pocket of her purse for her cell phone. No surprise to see the Lark Song Inn on her caller ID. A manager's job was never done. "Let me guess. The computer system froze up again."

"Good guess." It was her boss and the owner of the inn, Cady Winslow. "But after crashing twice this morning, the computer has given up the fight and has accepted it is going to have to talk with the printer."

"Maybe it's a lover's quarrel. Now they have made up and all is well." Since she was in her purse, she dug out a few dollar bills. "Maybe it will be a happily-ever-after for the two of them."

"It had better be. If their differences of opinion last and they refuse to talk, a breakup may be pending. The printer might have to move out and we'll never see him again." Cady's sunny sense of humor made it easy to work for her. "I know you're on your break, but I'm taking off and I want to make sure you see this text. It's from my little goddaughter and I think it is about the cutest thing I've seen in a while."

"Send it."

"Here it is. I'll see you bright and early for the staff meeting tomorrow?"

"I'll be the one holding the jumbo-sized cup of coffee and yawning."

"Jumbo-sized coffee cups. I'll put that in my to-buy list." Laughing, Cady said goodbye and hung up.

"Here!" Something clattered and clanked, drawing her attention as she scrolled through her phone's list. Chloe held out her hand. "It will be a dollar fifty."

"Keep the change." Eloise handed over the bills and took the ice-cream cone thrust at her. She was trying to scroll through her phone at the same time, so she didn't instantly notice the ice cream was the wrong flavor.

"Hey, Chloe!" She hung out the window, but it was too late. No Chloe in sight. A tall, broad shouldered shadow crowned by a wide Stetson fell across the pavement. The shadow strolled closer accompanied by the substantial pad of a cowboy's confident gait as he moseyed into view.

Handsome.

"I think there was a mix-up," he said in a deep baritone, layered with warmth and humor. "The little waitress didn't look like she had things together. Is this yours?"

"Uh…" She might be able to answer him *if* she could rip her gaze away from the shaded splendor of his face.

That turned out to be nearly impossible. The strong, lean lines of his cheekbones, the sparkling blue eyes and the chiseled jaw held her captive. He looked vaguely familiar, but her neurons were too stunned to fire.

Wow. That was the only word her beleaguered brain could come up with. Wow. Wow. Wow.

"I think the car-hop girl is new at this." He swaggered over with an athletic, masculine gait.

If only his drop-dead gorgeous smile wasn't so amazing, her command of the English language might have a chance of returning. She might be able to agree with him or at least point out that Chloe was simply being Chloe.

"You didn't order a chocolate ice-cream cone?" He was near enough now that she could see the crystal blue sparkles in his irises and the smooth texture of his shaven jaw. The gray T-shirt he wore clung to muscled biceps.

Again, wow. Fortunately, the power of thought returned to her brain and she was able to move her mouth and emit a semblance of an intelligent word or two. "I did. This must be yours."

"Guilty."

"Pink ice cream. Really?" She felt a smile stretch the corners of her mouth. She arched one brow as she held out the paper-wrapped cone.

"Hey, it's strawberry, not pink." His chuckle was brief but it rumbled like dreams. He plucked the cone out of her hand and offered her the chocolate one. "That looks good. I thought about keeping it. Tell me something."

"I'm not sure that I should." She daintily licked the cone before it decided to start dripping.

"Why do you look familiar?" He leaned back against the steel arm holding the speaker and menu. "I've seen you somewhere before."

"I thought the same thing." Looking up at him with the dark Stetson shading his face and bright sunshine framing him in the background, the realization struck her like a falling meteor. She had not only seen him before, she knew him. She remembered a younger version of the handsome cowboy on the back of a horse riding through town years ago before she left town, attending the church service in a suit and tie, and in the back of the Grangers' pickup as they motored away from the diner. "You're Sean, one of Cheyenne's cousins."

"You know Cheyenne?"

"We've been best friends since kindergarten." Long distances could not change true friendship. "I'm the one with the white mare. Cheyenne and I used to always go riding."

"Now I remember." He took a bite of ice cream and nodded, his bright blue gaze traveling over her as he considered the past. "You have a gorgeous horse. Almost as fast as Cheyenne's girl."

"On the right day, sometimes she was faster. She still is." A drip landed on her knuckle, reminding her she was holding ice cream, which was obviously starting to melt. "What are you doing this far south? Don't you live with your family up near Buffalo?"

"Used to, but they tossed me out of the nest. My dad wanted me to get my master's, but I've been begging my uncle Frank for a job for years. He finally gave in."

"That's hard to believe."

"I know, that's what I tell him every day. But I'm determined not to be a disappointment." He winked, his easygoing humor only making him more attractive. He gave off the aura of a man confident of his masculinity so he didn't need to flaunt it.

"I wasn't talking about your work, I was wondering why you turned down the chance for more schooling? Why would you choose to live in Wild Horse?"

"Why not? What's not to like?" Dimples flirted with the corners of his chiseled mouth. "Clean air, more freedom than a guy knows what to do with and I get to ride my horse every day all day. There's nothing better than that."

"You are highlighting only the good parts." Why was she smiling? She simply could not seem to stop. His grin was infectious and, to make matters worse, sweet little bubbles began effervescing in her stomach. "It's an hour drive to see a movie or shop in a mall. Nothing ever happens here. Everyone knows your business."

"I don't mind all that one bit." His baby blues twinkled charmingly and made the pops in her stomach multiply.

She wasn't attracted to the man, was she? Goodness. She shook her head, determined to keep that from happening. "Then you are right where you should be. I'm currently suffering from urban withdrawal, but it's slowly getting better."

"Urban? Where?" He tilted his head a notch, leaning a fraction closer to her as if he were interested in her answer.

"Seattle." She took a swipe of ice cream before it melted and tumbled off the cone. "Where did you go to school?"

"Seattle Christian University." He chuckled. "I can't believe we used to live in the same city. Cheyenne should have mentioned it."

"She's had a lot on her mind going to vet school." Intrigued, Eloise forgot about the tingles in her tummy and the fact that the man's handsomeness pulled at her with all the gravitational force of a black hole. "Where did you live?"

"In an apartment just off Fremont Avenue. How about you?"

"I rented a house with some friends a few blocks off 45th."

"Not far away at all, not really, and we didn't even know it. How about that?" Sean leaned back, a deliberately casual movement and yet the power of his gaze remained locked on hers and made the world fade away. The distant *clomp, clomp* of Chloe's skates, the nicker from one of the ponies, the sun's heat and the whine of the car's struggling air conditioning all turned to silence.

An electronic ring shattered the moment, time rolled forward and the sounds of the hot May day returned. Chloe clomped up on her skates. "Oops. I saw you two across the lot exchanging cones. Did I make a mistake?"

"Don't worry about it," Sean said breezily as he tugged a cell from his pocket.

The girls on ponies rode leisurely by, licking ice-cream cones. A diesel truck rumbled along on the street behind her and a second electronic chime came from the phone she didn't even remember tossing onto the passenger seat. Right next to her cane.

Her cane. She stared at the snazzy pink length of metal—she'd gone for the bright, cheerful color hoping to jazz up the fact of her disability—and the fizz evaporated from her stomach. The smile died on her lips. She knew full well Sean Granger hadn't spotted her cane in her car or he never would have taken the time to talk with her. This she knew from personal experience.

She glanced at the screen, where the text her boss had sent her was overlaid by Cheyenne's cell number. She considered answering it, but then she would wind up saying where she was and what she was doing, and it would be impossible not to mention the handsome man chatting amicably on his phone a few feet away. No, best to hit the ignore button and get back to her friend later.

"Well, duty calls." Sean pushed away and offered her a dashing grin, making time stand still. Again. Her neurons forgot how to fire. Again. She sat captivated by the wholesome goodness of the man as he tipped his hat to her. "I'll see you around, Eloise Tipple."

"Bbb—" The closest thing she could manage to good-bye, but he didn't seem to notice her jumbled attempt at speech. He loped away with a relaxed, confident stride and hopped into his truck.

"Do you think he was mad at me?" Chloe spoke up, startling Eloise completely. The phone tumbled out of her grip and hit the floor. The teenager scrunched her face up with worry. "Are you? I couldn't believe I got your ice-cream cone wrong. My manager is right. One order at a time. I'm no good with two."

"It's not a big deal." As the truck motored away and took Sean with it, her neurons began to fire normally. Her vocabulary returned. "Have a good day, Chloe."

"I will, now the lunch rush is nearly over. Bye!"

It wasn't until Eloise had pulled onto the street heading away from town that it struck her. Sean Granger had remembered her name.

Chapter Two

Find homeless horses, Eloise scribbled onto her to-do list. This was her new assignment, added to all the others. Her desk at the inn was tucked a few steps down the hallway from the front desk. Her only window gazed out at the new rose gardens and gave a peek at the new stable. Cady wanted to offer horses for the guests to ride and that meant someone had to find the appropriate animals. That someone was her. Eloise took a sip of bottled water and smiled at the text message shining on her phone's luminous screen.

> Aunt Cady, you promised to get your horses from the shelter. You have to save their lives so they can have a home and be loved.

Eloise sighed. Cady's little goddaughter's message was too cute, but how did one go about finding homeless horses? Did the county humane society take them in? There was only one way to find out. She grabbed the yellow pages out of her bottom desk drawer and began leafing through it. *If the phone book doesn't help, then Lord please send a hint or two to guide me.*

The bell above the front door chimed and the telltale snap of sandals on the polished hardwood had her rising to her feet. She grabbed her cane and tapped around the corner, expecting to see the Neilsons, who were yet to arrive for their reservation. So when she saw a tall, slender young woman with auburn hair and smiling eyes wearing a Washington State University shirt and denim cutoffs, she let out a surprised squeal. "Cheyenne!"

"It wouldn't have been a surprise if you checked the message I left you." She threw out her arms wide for a welcoming hug then stepped back, squinting. "You look good. Really good. How's the pain level?"

"Better. How does it feel to finally be a vet?" Eloise led the way toward the comfortable sitting area near the front desk.

"I start working for Nate next Monday, and I still can't believe this is really happening. You would have thought graduation might have made it clear to me." She shook her head, bouncing along, full of exuberance. "I'm jazzed. I can't wait to start."

"When did you get back in town?"

"Last night much later than I'd meant to. What are you doing after work?"

"Nothing exciting."

"Want to grab dinner at Clem's?"

The phone rang before she could answer, so Eloise grabbed it at the front desk. The Neilsons had landed at the airport one town away and wanted to verify their directions. Simple enough to make sure they were heading the right way. Eloise got their cell number in case they didn't show up in an hour, kept the cordless phone with her and leaned on her cane. "Want an iced latte?"

"Do you have to ask?"

They changed directions and headed for the dining

room, which was nearly empty. The lunch crowd had gone and the early diners wouldn't start showing up for a few hours. Pleasant clinks and clanks from the kitchen rang like discordant music.

"So, is that yes for dinner at Clem's?" Cheyenne chose a table near a sunny window. "Or is the diner too common for you, now that you work in such a fancy place?"

"Are you kidding? I'm a diner gal through and through."

"Me, too. I'm way underdressed for this dining room." Cheyenne plucked at the collar of her T-shirt. "It's a good thing I have an in with the manager."

"Exactly, or we would toss your kind out." It was fun to banter. A great perk to being home was seeing old friends. She leaned her cane against the window sill and settled into the cushioned chair.

"You look good. How is the physical therapy coming along?"

"It's done. My leg has come as far as it can." She shrugged one shoulder, as if that wasn't a big deal. As if she didn't feel torn apart every time she said it. Life dealt you hard blows and you had to deal and keep moving forward. That's what she decided in the ambulance when she was being rushed to the trauma center. She'd known before the firemen had cut her out of the car that life would never be the same. The paralysis had improved but not disappeared, which was amazing enough. "I can ride my horse. That's the good news. I can't complain. Now, down to business. Are you ever going to tell me what really happened with Edward?"

"I told you, he thought I was getting too serious so he broke things off." Cheyenne rolled her eyes and turned her attention to Sierra, who bounded over in her black-

and-white uniform. Cheyenne lit up. "Hey, I heard a rumor you're marrying my brother. Nice engagement ring."

"Shocking, but true. When he asked, I accepted." Sierra radiated happiness. "I don't know what came over me."

"I can't imagine," Cheyenne agreed. After they ordered and Sierra disappeared into the kitchen, she propped both elbows on the table and rested her chin on her hands. "So, what's new with you?"

"With me? I'm not buying the innocent look. I know exactly what you're doing."

"What am I doing? I'm just sitting here."

Eloise wished she could make her friend's pain disappear. Anyone looking at Cheyenne wouldn't guess she was nursing a broken heart. "You and Edward broke up on Valentine's Day. That's three months ago. You aren't over it, I can tell."

"I've decided to stay in denial. It isn't just a river in Egypt." Cheyenne waggled her brows.

"That isn't funny enough to distract me, and you know how I like to laugh." Eloise stretched out her bad leg and relaxed against the chair cushions. "You forget I have a romantic disaster in my past, so I know how it can feel when some guy who says he loves you up and ends things."

"Our relationship was convenient for him, that was all." Cheyenne's face tightened, although she acted light and breezy as if she hadn't been devastated. "I'm over it."

"Wow, your denial is really strong."

"It's made out of titanium. Nothing will crack it."

"Then I guess we'd better change the subject."

"Fabulous idea."

And she knew exactly what the subject would be. The handsome cowboy from the drive-in flashed into her mind. In truth, he hadn't ever really gone away but lurked in the back of her brain like a happy thought. "I ran into your cousin in town today. He has an affinity for ice-cream cones, too."

"Right. Sean. I'm trying to remember the last time you saw him."

"Years and years ago. Probably the summer before we graduated from high school, the last summer I was home." She caught sight of Sierra returning and debated changing the subject. But why? It wasn't as if she were interested in Sean Granger. Besides, she wanted to know more about him. "He's changed. I hardly recognized him."

"He's gotten tall, hasn't he? I think he's taller than Dad."

Sierra set the glasses of icy drinks on the table. "Are you talking about Sean? He's such a nice guy. It's too bad what happened to him."

"Why? What happened?" Inquiring minds wanted to know. She leaned forward, her heart rate tapping inexplicably faster.

"Bad breakup." Sierra added two rolls of cloth napkins to the table. "She shattered his heart, or so I hear. She up and started dating someone else."

Images of the handsome cowboy hopped into Eloise's mind. Of the black Stetson shading his rugged face, the dimples bracketing his grin and the strong dependability the man exuded. "He didn't look too heartbroken to me."

"Are you kidding? It's a Granger family trait not to deal with emotions." Cheyenne took a sip of her iced coffee. "I notice you are doing the same thing, Eloise."

"Me?" She smiled at Sierra as the waitress padded away, knowing she was completely guilty. But did she want to talk about it?

No. Not in this lifetime. The cane leaning against the windowsill was proof. There was no sense crying over what you could not change. "Isn't that like the pot calling the kettle black?"

"Absolutely." Cheyenne smiled and lifted her glass for a toast. "Here's to denial and burying emotions."

"It is the only way to go."

With a laugh, they clinked glasses and the conversation turned to the evening's plans, Eloise's search for horses and Cheyenne's funny tales of her long drive home from vet school.

This was the life. Sean Granger popped the top on the cold can of root beer, waving goodbye to the housekeeper who had left dinner in the oven and the timer set. All he had to do was listen for the ding. Mrs. Gunderson waved back as she hurried around the corner of the house and disappeared, leaving him blissfully alone. Well, almost alone. A clunk on the other side of the screen door reminded him two Grangers still remained in the house. But not for much longer.

He ambled over to the porch swing and settled onto the cushion to watch the sunset. Comfortable. *Thanks for leading me here, Lord. It's just where I want to be in life.* He took a sip of his soda. A cow grazing on the other side of a white fence leaned over the top board and mooed at him. Her bright brown eyes were focused on his soda can.

"Buttercup!" The screen door whispered open and

the youngest Granger sister popped out. Addison slung her designer bag over her shoulder. "You can't have fizzy drinks. They give you the burps. Remember?"

The cow's long sorrowful moo may have been a comment that some pleasures were worth a little discomfort.

"Dad should just let that cow live in the house like a dog, she's so spoiled." Addy winked as she waltzed by him. "It's Friday night. You shouldn't be here alone. I can stay with you and keep watch on Sunny. I'm worried about her."

"No way. Don't you change your plans. I can keep an eye on your expecting mare. Besides, I want to spend the evening with my sweetie." He stretched out his legs and crossed them at the ankles.

Buttercup, his sweetie, mooed again as if in total agreement.

"Then enjoy the peace and quiet while you can." Addy's advice was delivered with a grin as she hopped down the steps, strawberry blond hair flying behind her, looking a lot like his baby sister as she hurried enthusiastically down the concrete path. "Don't forget to do your own dishes!"

"I know. My mom trained me right," he called after her as she disappeared around the corner.

"That's debatable." A different voice answered. Cheyenne pushed open the screen door. "I saw the state of your bedroom. Do you know how to pick up anything?"

"Hey, that's my private domain. I know how to do housework, but I'm not so good at doing it without someone telling me to." He may as well be honest. He'd learned that was the best way to go through life, even if he could think of folks who didn't agree—like his former fiancée.

"That's a tad better than my brothers." Cheyenne jingled her truck keys in one hand. "Are you really going to stay here all by your lonesome? It's Friday night."

"I didn't know I'd be here alone, but yeah, I don't mind. I like the peace." It was what he preferred, and he'd had enough drama with Meryl to last him a lifetime. He liked quiet. He liked computers, books and watching time go by.

"It's weird now that Dad's with Cady." Cheyenne hesitated on the steps. "He used to be home every weekend night unless there was something going on at the church. Now, look. I never thought it would happen, but he's dating."

"He sure is. He trailered up his horse and drove off about an hour ago. Said he and Cady were going for a ride. He looked pleased as punch." Sean took another sip of root beer and let the feather-light summery air puff over him.

"What about you?" Cheyenne twisted around to walk backwards. "There's no one you have your eye on?"

"Who? Me?" He stared off into the distance. The cow was going to hurt herself straining over the fence like that. He climbed to his feet, doing his level best not to think of pretty Eloise. "No. I'm done with relationships. They're for the birds."

"I know the feeling." Cheyenne seemed satisfied at last, and he realized she didn't want him to feel alone. That would explain why she was hesitating.

"What are you up to?" He set aside his can.

"I'm having dinner with a friend. Wait, you know her. Eloise, remember? We've been friends forever."

"Blond hair, green eyes, is real quiet?" Surprising

how the mention of her could make him smile. "Saw her today at the Steer In."

"Yes. That's Eloise. She's home to stay, just like I am, so we're celebrating with cheeseburgers and chocolate milkshakes. I can bring you an order home."

"No. Mrs. G. left me on casserole duty. She's got the timer set and a salad in the fridge." He ambled down the steps and dug into his jeans pocket. The cow, scenting the molasses treat he found, hopped up and down excitedly. "Eloise is the one who used to skate, right?"

"Ice dancing. She won two world championships." Cheyenne nodded as she hesitated at the corner of the garage.

A long span of mown grass separated them, and he had to speak up to be heard above the mooing cow and the twitter of larks. "What happened? Did she get injured or something? I saw a cane in her car."

"She was in a serious car accident." Cheyenne frowned, sad for her friend. "It's amazing she walks, but she'll never skate professionally again."

Emotion punched him in the gut, reminding him life could be a tough road. He handed over the molasses treat and gave Buttercup a pat as she chewed happily. Sunshine gleamed off the cow's sleek black coat. Her pure white face and white tipped ears made her look as cute as a button. He thought of Eloise and couldn't guess what it would be like to lose a goal like that, although he knew what tragedy felt like. His older brother Tim, an Army Ranger, had been killed in action. The family had gone on but the loss had marked them all.

"Oops! I'm late." Cheyenne darted around the corner and out of sight, her words carrying to him on the breeze. "If you change your mind, you have my cell number. Keep a close eye on Sunny and if you think she's not doing all right, call."

"I know the drill," he told Buttercup as he rubbed her nose.

She gazed up at him with puppy-dog eyes, sank her teeth into his hat and lifted it off his head.

"Funny girl." He rescued it from her and dug another treat out of his pocket. Life was good on the Wyoming range, and he was glad to be a carefree bachelor in command of his life. So what if it got a little lonely? He could handle that. If the thought of Eloise Tipple's lovely face made him reconsider, he had to admit he was lonelier than he'd thought. It wasn't easy being a lone wolf.

"Don't look at me like that," he admonished Buttercup. "I really am a lone wolf."

The cow shook her head as if she didn't believe him for a second.

"Is that you, honey?"

"Yes, Mom." Eloise tapped through the shadowy kitchen and pushed open the back screen. The music of the nearby river serenaded her as she stepped onto the patio.

Helene Tipple looked up from her cross-stitch piece. "Did you have a good time catching up with Cheyenne?"

"I did." She leaned her cane against the patio table and eased into a cushioned seat. Another positive about being back—there was no place like home. Their conversation had covered everything essential while neatly skipping the painful. "Cheye and I are going riding this week. I get to go over to the ranch and see all the new foals."

"That's nice, dear." Mom poked her needle through the embroidery hoop and fussed with the stitch. "I was talking with your grandma today."

"You talk with her every day." Eloise rolled her eyes, already bracing herself. She knew exactly what her mom was going to say because they'd had this conversation many times before. "She told you about my upcoming blind date, didn't she?"

"She is pretty excited about this young man. She wants you to call her. Take a few moments to gather your strength first." Mom's eyes twinkled as if she were enjoying herself.

"Yes, because this is so amusing." Eloise shook her head, laughing, too. "This is my life. My grandmother is finding dates for me."

"And don't you disappoint her." Dad spoke up with a rattle of his magazine page and a grin.

"I wouldn't dream of it." She loved her grandmother with all her heart. No one on earth wanted to disappoint Gran. "Even if she is torturing me."

Her parents chuckled as if she'd made a joke. Sure, her personal life was a laugh a minute. Shaking her head and laughing at herself—what else was a girl to do?—she hoisted up out of the extremely comfortable chair and made her way to the kitchen. As she dialed the phone, her gaze drifted to the large picture window overlooking the patio. Her parents made an iconic picture, sitting side by side beneath the striped table umbrella. Their silence was a contented one, broken by quiet murmurings and gentle smiles, a sign of their long and happy marriage.

Not everyone got the fairy tale. That was simply a plain fact. Eloise leaned against the counter and listened to the phone ring.

"Hello?" Gran warbled cheerfully. "Is that you, Eloise? Your mama promised you would be calling me."

"Yes, it's me, Gran." Theirs was a lifetime love, too. She adored her grandmother. She would do anything for her, which was why she was doomed. "You might as well get to the point."

"I talked with Madge." Gran's excitement vibrated across the line. "This is what I learned about George. He manages an office-supply store over in Sunshine. He's a good Christian boy and he wants to get married."

"Why can't he find someone to marry him who actually knows him?"

"Well, he is terribly short but you don't mind that, do you? A short husband is better than none at all. It's what's inside that counts."

"Yes, it is." Who was she to be arguing with that? She leaned her cane against the cabinet doors and prayed for fortitude.

"I have high hopes for this one. Don't worry, I'm looking out for you, sweetheart."

"I'm looking out for you too, Gran. I'll drop by after work tomorrow." Her grandmother needed a little help around the house these days, and she was happy to do it. That way they could spend quality time together, another very big advantage to being back home again.

After chatting for a few more minutes, she bid Gran goodbye and hung up the phone. The peace of the evening filled the kitchen like the rosy light of the sunset tumbling from the western horizon. The entire landscape glowed as if painted with a luminous pearled paint. Her mind drifted back over her very good day and lingered on the memory of a man with a black Stetson holding a strawberry ice-cream cone in one rugged hand. A very nice image, indeed.

Chapter Three

"Good afternoon. Lark Song Inn." Eloise tucked the receiver between her chin and shoulder. "How may I help you?"

"Yeah, this is Nate Cannon. I need to talk with Eloise."

"Dr. Cannon." The local vet. A kick of anticipation charged through her, so she grabbed a pen off the front desk and poised it over the memo pad. "I'm Eloise. Did you happen to hear about my mission?"

"Cheyenne clued me in. She said you folks are looking to buy horses in need, and I happen to know of a pair."

"Bless you." She'd tried the local agencies and organizations over the last handful of days, but no luck. "Where are they? What are they like?"

"Two geldings, as gentle as could be. Their owner passed away a while back and the folks who inherited the land don't want to keep them. It's hard to sell horses this old, so if your boss is looking to make a difference in an animal's life, she wouldn't regret taking them in."

"They sound perfect." The poor things. She glanced

at her watch. Wendy should be back from her break in a few minutes. "Could I take a look this afternoon?"

"I'll give you the address and phone number. Now, these folks aren't the most agreeable so you might want to bring someone with you who really knows horses. Like Cheyenne. I'd offer, but I've got a show horse with colic to get back to and a busy afternoon after that. You could call my receptionist. She might be able to book you a time."

"Thanks, but I'll call Cheyenne." After getting the necessary information, she buzzed Cady, who was delighted at the prospect of horses for the stables, then dialed her best friend's number.

"Hello?" A familiar baritone rumbled across the line. "Stowaway Ranch."

"Is this Sean?" Why was she smiling? The man simply had that effect on her. She was curious. That was different from interested.

"Eloise. How are you doing?"

"Fine enough." Was it her imagination or did he sound glad to hear from her?

"Are you calling for Cheyenne?"

"Guilty. She promised me use of her horse expertise. Tell me she's there."

"I wish I could but she took off to do some shopping in Sunshine. Should be gone all afternoon. I might not be an expert when it comes to horses, but I'm no slouch either. What kind of help do you need?"

"Uh…" Brilliant answer. Her brain decided to short circuit again. "The vet found some horses."

"Oh, and you need someone to go with you. I can do that."

"Uh…" Was she stuck on that word? What was the matter with her?

"It's a slow afternoon and I like to make myself useful. I can bring a horse trailer."

"I can't say no to that." Especially since she didn't own a vehicle capable of pulling one. But did she really want to spend an afternoon with the most gorgeous man she'd ever met? She was fairly sure judging by the amount of friendliness in his voice that he hadn't noticed her cane yet. She dreaded the moment when he did, but putting horses in the inn's stables was her new assignment. She wanted to do her job well. "Let me give you the address."

"Great. I need something to write with." A drawer banged open before he came back on the line. "Got it."

"You probably know where this is already, but the vet gave me detailed instructions." She gave him the information. "When can you get there?"

"Give me thirty minutes?"

"Thirty minutes it is. Thanks for helping out, Sean."

"Hey, that's what friends are for." He set down the pen and folded the scrap of paper.

"I didn't know we were friends."

"A friend of Cheyenne's is a friend of mine." He ignored Mrs. Gunderson who bustled into sight with a laundry basket balanced on one hip. A lone wolf could have a friend or two and still be a lone wolf, right? "I'm happy to help. I like what Cady's doing. She could be filling her stalls with pampered horses, but she wants to make a difference. I'll see you soon."

"Thanks, Sean." Eloise's gentle alto was about the prettiest sound he'd ever heard. She wasn't fake, like some women he could think of—Meryl came to mind— but honest and sincere. He liked that. Those were just the right qualities for a friend.

He hung up and caught Mrs. Gunderson's raised eyebrow as she paused midway up the stairs, free hand on the rail. There was no mistaking that motherly look.

"What?" He held up both hands, the innocent man that he was. "I didn't do anything."

"I didn't say a thing." She had raised five sons of her own, so he knew she was wise to the ways of the male mind. "You call me if you aren't coming home for supper."

"Why wouldn't I be home for supper?" He grabbed a chocolate-chip cookie from the jar. "This isn't a date. It's a humanitarian mission. Well, an animal welfare mission."

"You like that girl." Mrs. G. narrowed her gaze at him. "Don't try and fool me."

"I'm not fooling you. I like her. What's not to like? But I don't *like* her." After Meryl, he'd be stupid to. A smart man would be leery after being used like that.

"Sometimes the best things come along when we aren't looking for them." She went on her way, padding up the stairs and out of sight, her words carrying up to him. *"All things are possible to him who believes."*

Boy, did she have the wrong idea. Sean shook his head. Mrs. G. couldn't be more mistaken. When he wiped a crumb off his shirt, he noticed his T-shirt had a hole in it. His jeans sported grass stains and his work boots were dirty.

Maybe he'd better go change. Getting spiffed up had nothing to do with seeing Eloise. It was simply a matter of cleanliness. He took the stairs two at a time, whistling.

"This must be the place," Eloise said to herself as she glanced at the reflective numbers stuck to the side of a

battered black mailbox. Although two numerals were
missing, the description matched the vet's directions so
she eased her car off the paved county road and onto a
driveway that was more dirt and potholes than gravel.
She listened to the rush and whap of weeds and grass
growing in the center of the lane hitting the underside
of her car. Hopefully there wasn't anything big enough
to do any damage. She gripped the steering wheel tight
and eased up on the gas pedal.

Something dark and large lumbered up behind her,
filling the reflective surface of her rearview mirror. She
recognized that dark blue pickup. Sean. The sunshine
seemed brighter, although that was probably an illu-
sion and had nothing to do with the man's appearance.
She eased around a hairpin corner and a dilapidated
covering built out of corrugated metal and weathered
two-by-fours came into sight. It huddled sadly against
a broken-down fence. Barbed wire hung dangerously
from listing and rotting posts. Most of the grass had
been eaten away from an acre-sized field, where two
horses pricked their ears, spotted the truck and came
running.

She pulled to a stop in front of a carport that had seen
better days. A rusty truck rested in the shade. Overgrown grass danced in the wind as she watched Sean's
vehicle pull up beside her. Maybe the last wheeze of the
air conditioner was the reason the hair stood up on her
arms. She did not want it to be a reaction to the man
strolling into sight. She braced herself for the inevitable
and reached for her cane.

Sean Granger looked like a western hero in his long-
legged worn blue jeans. The white T-shirt he wore emphasized his sun-kissed tan and as he swept off his
Stetson, muscles rippled beneath the knit cotton blend.

He raked one hand through his brown hair and smiled down at her as he opened her car door. His dreamy blue eyes captured her with a steady stare and then his gaze slid downward as she climbed out from behind the wheel, stood tall and used her cane.

Here was where he dimmed down the smile and his friendliness when he got a good look at her cane. It's what most guys did whether they were interested or not. She braced herself for it as she took one limping step, but it didn't come. Instead Sean closed the door for her, nodding toward the horses. "Did you get a look at them?"

"No, I was too busy trying not to lose my car in one of the potholes," she quipped and was rewarded with a grin as he swept his hat back on.

"They saw the truck and came running. Look at them." His hand settled on the curve of her shoulder, a friendly weight, as he turned her gently toward the fence line. "I wonder if their former owner drove a truck like mine."

"They keep staring at it, almost waiting for someone else who might be in there." She gasped, realizing how they must be feeling. "Dr. Cannon didn't say how long the gentleman who owned them has been gone."

"Three months. Animals don't forget those they love." Sean ambled up to the fence and held out his hands for the horses to scent.

She took the opportunity to put a little physical distance between them. He was more touchy-feely than she was used to or felt comfortable with. "How do you know that?"

"Uncle Frank knew. I told him where I was headed. He knows everyone in these parts." Sean patted one of the horses. The big black gelding lowered his head for a good ear scratch. No one had taken time to comb out the tangles and burrs in his mane, and his hooves needed attention.

"You are a good fellow," Sean mumbled and the horse closed his eyes in trust. There was something deeply calming about the man, Eloise agreed. He made others feel safe.

"Are you the folks the vet called about?" A middle-age man wearing faded overalls and carrying a pipe limped into sight. He didn't seem to be in good health.

"We are." She spun to face him, thinking about the blank check her boss had handed over to her. "I'm Eloise from the Lark Song Inn."

"I'm Harry." He tipped his sagging hat. "Are you still interested now that you've seen them? They ain't much, and I regret to say I'm not up to caring for them."

"I'm sure we can settle on a price." She glanced over her shoulder at the horses, one still accepting strokes from Sean, the other watching the blue pickup sadly. He finally lowered his head, perhaps realizing his beloved former owner would not be emerging from the pickup, and stood still and silent, his dejection as tangible as the wind on her face.

She couldn't bring back to them what was lost, but she could make sure these horses were cherished and pampered. Good things were ahead for them. They just didn't know it yet. She tugged the check out of her purse, wondering how best to proceed.

"Do you trust me?" Sean towered over her, as breathtaking as any hero in a Western legend. "I can negotiate for you, if you'd like."

"Yes, thank you." She handed him the check, relieved in more ways than she knew how to say. She had no idea what the horses were worth, and she could see the man had a tough row to hoe. She didn't know what was fair, but she sensed Sean knew how to make it right.

She watched him stride away and offer Harry his hand. They shook, making introductions and small talk about the man who was deceased. A low-throated nicker caught her attention, and she found the friendlier horse watching her with curious eyes.

"Your lives are about to improve." She ran her fingertips down the gelding's graying nose. "Just you wait and see."

In the back lot at the inn Sean lowered the ramp with a clatter, surprised as Eloise tapped up the incline with a lead rope in hand. She didn't let her cane slow her down much. A glow of admiration filled him as he followed her up. The horses, not used to the trailer, were in various stages of fear. The black one fidgeted against his gate.

Eloise laid a comforting hand on his flank and spoke calmly and confidently like someone who had been around horses all her life. "It's going to be all right, Licorice."

The gelding blew out a breath, as if he were highly doubtful of that.

"How about you, Hershey?" she asked, unlatching the brown gelding's gate. The bay glanced over his shoulder to study her, his eyes white-rimmed, but he didn't move much as Eloise clipped into his halter and led him out.

Why couldn't he look away? He ought to be paying attention to the horses, but all he saw was the woman. She walked like a ballerina even with an obvious limp.

There was strength and a beauty inside her that became clearer every time he looked.

"I know you're worried, Hershey, but trust me when I say you have one of the best stalls in the county waiting for you." Her alto rose and fell like a song over the pad of her cane and the clomp of hooves on the ramp. "Cady went all out when she built this stable. Every stall is huge and it has a view. That's it. Turn for me, big guy. Come this way, that's right."

Kindness made a woman truly beautiful, Sean decided as he laid a hand on the black's neck. The gelding shivered, lunging nervously against the metal barrier.

"It's all right," he crooned, aware of the tension bunching in the horse's muscles. "It has to be hard having no say in this, but you are going to be just fine. No worries, buddy."

He clipped on the lead and backed the horse down the ramp. Every step Licorice took was halting as if he wanted to bolt into the trailer and go home. The unknown can be scary, so Sean used his voice to reassure the horse and led him down the breezeway between large but empty box stalls.

All he had to do was follow Eloise's voice, which felt as natural as breathing. Sunlight found her, burnishing her blond hair and haloing her like a Renaissance painting. Her frilly blouse and slacks weren't typical barn wear, but she didn't look out of place as she secured the gate to the straw-strewn stall. Inside, Hershey gave a snort and paraded around, taking in his view of the grassy paddock and various troughs for water, grain and alfalfa.

"Licorice can have the corner stall." She spotted him coming and opened the gate wide. "Rocco, who's on barn duty, has everything ready for them."

Across the row, a gold-and-white mare raced in from her paddock and clattered to a stop in her stall. Curious to meet her new neighbors, she arched her neck, whinnying in a friendly manner. Her big chocolate eyes shone a welcome.

"This is an exciting day for Misty, since she's been all alone in the stable," Eloise explained as he closed the gate and unhooked the lead.

"It's a pretty good day for me, too," he quipped, not at all sure how to say what he was feeling. "We did good work today."

"Yes, and I am indebted to you, sir." She handed him back the rope she'd used on Hershey. "I couldn't have done this without help."

"You mean without me."

"Well, yes, since you're the one who helped me." She gave her shiny hair a toss behind her shoulder, shaking her head at him as if she didn't know what to make of him. "It was good of you to volunteer. Cheyenne doesn't know what she missed out on. Until next time, that is."

"Hey, I don't mind doing this again." He kept his tone casual and made sure he didn't make eye contact. A lone wolf didn't work at making connections, he kept things light and loose. "I had fun. There's a lot of satisfaction to this. These horses weren't wanted, and now they are. It's a good way to spend an afternoon."

"So, you're really volunteering for next time?"

"Absolutely. Might as well make myself useful. Besides, Cheyenne might be busy and I have lots of spare time."

"Doesn't Frank keep you busy at the ranch?" Her grin hitched up in the corners of her soft mouth.

Cute. He ambled down the aisle at her side. "Sure.

I get in a hard day's work. Lately, my personal life has been a bit slow. That's the way I want to keep it."

"Me, too." Was that a hint of sorrow turning her gorgeous eyes a deep, emerald green?

Hard to tell because it was gone as quickly as it came. "That is, if you want me to lend a hand. You know I come with a horse trailer, right?"

"I know." She rolled her eyes at him.

Cuter. "Then you aren't agreeing to this reluctantly?"

"I am." She leaned her head back and gazed up into his eyes full on, a spark of humor lighting her up. "I am very reluctant about you."

"Sure, cuz most folks are." He smiled all the way down to his toes. It was nice being with her. They emerged through the open double doors into the kiss of the late-May sun and heat. Larks warbled, robins swooped by and a sparrow up on the roof chirped at them warningly. Grass whispered in the wind, leaves rustled and he couldn't remember the last time he felt so good.

"My dad didn't want me to grow up to be a cowboy, you know." He knelt to put up the ramp, working quickly, hardly thinking about it. He finished the quick task with a rattle and clang. "Said it was hard work and a hard life. He wanted something more for me."

"Is that why he didn't stay and help Frank with the ranching?"

"Yep, but I guess he didn't have the calling. Ranching is in my blood. That's why I'm here."

"Sometimes you get blessed with the right path to follow in life." The wind tangled her sleek blond locks. Again, that brief flash of sadness disappeared as if it had never been. "It doesn't always last, so you should enjoy it while you can."

"Good advice." He glanced at her cane, wondering if that's what life had taught her. He had some advice for her, too. "Sometimes you feel lost. When you look down, you realize you are already walking the path meant for you."

"You are a glass-is-half-full kind of man, aren't you?" She led the way down a garden walkway.

"Sure. It's a matter of choice. The glass has the same water in it either way." He flashed his dimples at her. "Let me guess. You're the kind who sees the glass as half-empty."

"I'm pleading the fifth." Dimples framed her smile, bright and merry.

The cutest yet. He jammed his hands into his pockets. "Speaking of glasses, I'm thirsty. How about we hunt down something cold to drink? My treat."

"No, that makes it a date." She grimaced in good humor. "Yikes. We probably don't want that. I'll get mine, you get yours."

"Wow, I guess I know where I stand," he quipped, following her down the breezeway.

"I've been on a lot of first dates lately. Did I sound defensive?"

"Only a little." He was glad to be with her. Eloise was fun and interesting. He was looking forward to finding out exactly how much.

Chapter Four

"Thank you, Sierra." Eloise lifted the iced coffee from the silver tray and took a cooling sip. Across from her on one of the inn's comfortable porch swings, Sean did the same.

"That engagement ring looks good on you," he told the waitress.

"Thanks. It's taken some getting used to." Sierra blushed rosily. Happiness radiated from her as she admired the impressive diamond on her left hand. "We have finally agreed on a July wedding."

"This is news." Sean leaned back, stretched his legs out and crossed them at the ankles. He was an interesting man to watch, all long, lean lines, strength and old-West charisma. "Tucker said you wanted to make sure not to interfere with Autumn's wedding next month."

"More like in three weeks. Haven't you noticed the flurry over it? You live in the same house." Sierra shook her head merrily as she padded away, off to wait on the Neilsons who were at the far end of the porch, holding hands and talking intimately.

"A bachelor tries to ignore all conversations, activities or magazines with the word 'wedding' in them," Sean quipped as he sipped at his coffee. "Self-preservation."

"Typical. I suppose you're the carefree-bachelor type. Never one to settle down." He was handsome enough to have his pick of women. "You probably left a dozen broken hearts behind when you moved here."

"Only one." His grin didn't lessen but the shine inside him did. His personality dimmed like a cloud passing before the sun. "And I didn't leave it behind. I brought it with me. It was mine."

"Yours?" He didn't look like a man with a broken heart. He certainly didn't act like one, not with his charm and easy humor. When she looked closer, emotion worked its way into the corner of his eyes, leaving attractive little crinkles. Perhaps he wasn't as easygoing as she first thought. She gave the swing a little push with her foot, setting it into motion. "Are you sure you weren't the one who did the breaking?"

"I was probably responsible for it." His confession rang low with truth and sincerity. He gave the appearance of a tough, untouchable man but she suspected his feelings ran deep. His grin was gone along with his easygoing manner, replaced by a solid realness that was attractive and manly. He swallowed hard before he spoke again. "I landed a good job at a software company. I was in management overseeing this great project, but I wasn't happy being trapped indoors all day."

"That can be hard for a country boy." She could picture it.

"I worked long hours, not that I mind hard work. I liked being a programmer, but I didn't love it. When Uncle Frank called on my birthday in February, I admitted to him that I would rather be in a saddle all day. That he had my ideal life."

"And he offered you a job?"

"He did. Temporary to start. To test the waters, he said, but I think he didn't want to upset my dad too much." He shrugged, glancing over his father's disappointment. He took another pull on the straw, letting the cool settle across his tongue and glide down his throat. It helped wash away the tough feelings he was trying to avoid. "I gave my notice and talked my folks into seeing the positive side of this. I was really psyched. Uncle Frank has a lot of land and livestock. This is a good opportunity for me to do what I love for a living. It was my decision that changed everything."

"What do you mean?"

"A special someone didn't want a blue-collar ranch hand for a husband." He may as well get it off his chest. "Meryl and I were engaged."

"Were?"

"She dumped me."

"Because you followed your dream?"

"That's the long and short of it." The country cliché was easier than admitting the truth. He'd loved Meryl. "I could have stayed, in fact I had the phone in hand to call Uncle Frank and decline his offer when I got the news she was already dating someone else and had been for a while. Hedging her bets, I think."

"I'm sorry. That had to have hurt."

"Yes." He swallowed hard against the pain, which was lessening. Mostly it was the humiliation that troubled him now. "I made a crucial mistake, but I learned a valuable lesson. Never fall in love with someone who doesn't love you the same way in return."

"I learned that hard lesson, too." She bit her bottom lip, the only sign of vulnerability he'd seen her make. With her classic good looks, smarts and kind personality he couldn't imagine she'd been through something similar.

"Who had the bad form not to care about you?" he wanted to know.

"Oh, he cared. Just not enough." Ghosts of pain darkened her green eyes and she shrugged one slender shoulder, as if she were well over it. No big deal.

He wasn't fooled. "Who was he?"

"My ice-dancing partner." She tore her gaze from his and stared out at the horizon, where the jagged peaks of the Tetons seemed to hold up the sky. "Cliché, I know. Gerald and I spent eight to ten hours a day together either on the ice or in the gym every day since I was eighteen. We even took classes together at the nearby university."

"You were truly close to him." He sympathized. He knew what that was like.

"I was." Shaky, she lifted the glass and sipped, still watching the white puffs of clouds in the pristine blue sky and the visual wonder of the Teton Range. Maybe she was trying to keep her emotions distant, too.

"You had been together a long time?" A question more than a statement, but he wanted it to sound casual, as if his pulse hadn't kicked up and he wasn't eager to know why she'd been hurt.

"We were friends for the first three years and then it turned into something more. Something really nice." Maybe she wasn't aware of how her voice softened and her expression grew lighter as if she'd had the rare chance to touch more than one dream. She sat up straighter and set her coffee on the nearby end table. "For a while it was sweet and comfortable and reassuring. He was there whenever I needed him, at least when we were skating partners."

"Sounds as if you two had a good bond." He couldn't say the same. He'd loved Meryl. He hated to admit he might still love her a little bit and against his will. But he'd never had that type of tie with her.

"It was nice." She might think she was hiding her sadness, but she would be wrong. "I guess some things aren't meant to last."

"What happened?"

"Are you telling me you can't guess?" She rubbed at her knee in small circles before turning away from him to fetch her drink. He didn't imagine the hurt in the silence that fell between them.

A car accident, Cheyenne had said. But it was far more serious than that.

"A drunk driver was going the wrong way on the floating bridge when I was coming home after a late night practicing for my church's Christmas pageant. I saw the lights and I tried to avoid him. But I steered toward the right hand shoulder, what little there was of it, and he decided to do the same. I spent the next few months in the hospital and the next year in a rehabilitation center in Los Angeles." She took a sip, letting the pain settle between them. "Gerald couldn't wait, he had to keep training, so he found another skating partner. It turned out my injury and the distance between Seattle and L.A. were problems too big to overcome and our bond faded."

"I'm sorry that happened to you." Sympathy, that was the only reason he reached over to lay his hand on hers. He cared, sure, but he was in control of his emotions. He didn't care for her *too* much. He willed his understanding into his touch. "It wasn't fair."

"Fair? No. God never promised this life would be fair." Her chin went up, not a woman to feel sorry for herself. "But there have been many blessings that have come my way. I survived the accident. I beat the odds to walk again. I'm really very blessed."

"Sure, I see that," he agreed. She was blessed in more ways than he had understood before. She had strength and faith enough not to let the unfairness of her accident and injuries embitter her spirit. It was hard not to like her more, and he twined his fingers through hers, holding on and not wanting to let go. When he gazed into her clear green eyes, a similar tug of emotion wrapped around him. "You've had some tough blows. First the accident, then the breakup."

"Gerald tried. I have to give him credit. In the end he chose someone else." Her fingers tightened on his, holding on to him, too. "Yes, it was his new skating partner."

"Did you feel passed over?" That was certainly how he felt.

"Yes. It was easy for Gerald to move on. Proof his heart wasn't in it as deeply as mine was." She smiled, a mix of poignance and beauty that made her compelling. "Life goes on."

"It does." He was lost in the moment gazing into her, and he couldn't remember the name of any woman previous. The brush of the breeze, the murmur of the other couple on the porch and the faint rasp of the rocking swing silenced. The world narrowed until there was only Eloise and her hand, so much smaller, tucked in his.

Footsteps vaguely drummed closer and a familiar woman's voice pierced into his thoughts, pushing back the boundaries of his world so that Eloise was no longer the center. Cady smiled down at him and she wasn't alone. Two dark-haired girls, one around ten with braided pigtails and the other a little older with a touch of disdain, stood by her.

"Are you boyfriend and girlfriend?" the youngest girl wanted to know.

"No." He abruptly sat up and whipped his hand away from Eloise's. He knew why the kid was asking. It looked as if they were, sitting together with hands linked and sharing secrets. Couples did that sort of thing. He noticed Eloise seemed uncomfortable, too. He caught Cady's curious look and set out to reassure her. "Just talking. That's all. I suppose you heard about the horses?"

"I found Eloise's message on my voice mail when I reached the airport. I had to pick up these two and their father." Cady was honorary family to the girls and their godmother. They all had been close when she'd lived in New York City. Cady gently steered the kids toward the steps. "I can't wait to see our new horses. I didn't think to ask if they were gentle or even trained."

"They appear to be." Eloise grappled for her cane. "Their previous owner took good care of them, rode them regularly and they are steady and gentle. With a little training, they should make good, reliable horses for guests to ride."

"Excellent. What a great job, Eloise." Cady beamed, her happiness evident, before leading the girls away. "Let's go see the horses that were saved because of you, Julianna Elizabeth Stone."

"Do we get to ride them?" the little girl wanted to know as she skipped down the steps, and Cady's answer was lost in a rising gust of warm wind.

"Well, I guess I had better get back to my desk." Eloise checked her watch and grabbed her cane. "I've got just enough of my day left to call the farrier. Tonight I have to get off work on time."

"Why's that?" He climbed to his feet and followed her along the porch.

"I've got a date tonight. A blind date." She let her tone say it all.

"Poor you. Who set you up?"

"My grandma." She liked that Sean opened the door for her and held it. He was a gentleman underneath his cowboy charm. She stepped into the air-conditioning with a sigh. "She is the only person I can't say no to."

"So you are stuck going out on a date when you don't want to date?"

"Exactly." She liked that he understood. Her own mother had little sympathy for the situation with her matchmaking grandma. "But it's only one dinner. I can suffer through anything for an hour or so, at least that's what I tell myself."

"Sure. Who is it with?"

"I don't know him. Some guy who lives in the next town over." She hesitated in the well-appointed lobby, where their paths would part. The front door loomed to the left, the hallway leading to her office to the right. Remembering what Julianna had said made her blush. She wasn't interested in Sean in that way. "The last thing I need is a boyfriend."

"Right, because who wants to be tied down like that?" He swept off his Stetson and raked a hand through his thick dark hair. "Who needs the heart-ache?"

"You said it." It was nice that they shared this common ground. Not wanting a repeat of earlier when he'd held her hand too long, she backed away. Maybe a no-physical-contact policy between them would be a good idea. "Thanks again, Sean."

"Any time. I'll see you on the next horse-gathering mission?"

"Absolutely." She spun on her heel so she couldn't be tempted to watch him walk away. So she couldn't be tempted to wonder why any woman would have chosen another man over him. He didn't even seem to notice her disability. He didn't treat her differently because of her limp. He had understood the devastation she'd felt after her accident and her breakup.

He was a nice guy. A really nice guy. That type of man was hard to find, which made her think about her impending date. She gripped her cane tightly and turned her thoughts to the evening ahead. *Please, Lord,* she prayed as she always did before one of Gran's fix-ups. *Let this blind date not be too uncomfortable.*

God hadn't answered that particular prayer yet, but there was always a first. She was determined to hold out hope.

"We have to fend for ourselves tonight." Uncle Frank looked up from his laptop on the kitchen table the moment Sean came through the door. "The girls are in Jackson trying on the dresses for Autumn's wedding and dragged Mrs. G. with them. I told her you and I could throw something on the barbecue or hit the diner. What do you say?"

"The diner." He'd just finished cleaning out three stables and feeding all the horses. That explained where Autumn was, who practically lived in the barns. "Where's Tucker?"

"His fiancée is cooking for him, but he didn't see fit to extend an invitation to us." Frank grinned and pushed away from the table. "Let me grab my hat and my keys. How did the horse rescue turn out?"

"Good. The inn has some gentle animals, and some good horses have a caring home." He turned on his heel and headed right back out the door.

"Then it's good news all around." Frank seemed in an unusually chipper mood but he didn't explain as he hopped down the steps. Buttercup dashed up to the fence and mooed, her bright eyes sparkling. "Hey, girl. I'll come see you later. How's that?"

A discontented moo trailed after them as they headed to the garage.

"Tucker's about ready to take possession of the land he bought." Frank hopped into the driver's seat of his big black pickup.

Sean climbed into the passenger seat and buckled in. He liked his uncle. He couldn't count the number of times Dad had said, "You remind me of my brother." Sean supposed he and Frank were alike in some ways. They both liked the outdoors, loved animals, had ranching in their blood. Sean liked to think he was as even-tempered. "Does that mean the Greens are officially moved off the land he bought?"

"They leave tomorrow for Florida. Retirement. I can't picture that." He started the engine and gunned down the driveway with the speed and skill of someone who had done it thousands of times. Trees whipped by along with rolling green fenced fields full of grazing horses. The view of the Tetons and the Wyoming sky could knock the breath out of you. Frank turned the truck onto the paved county road. "I'm going to wind up like my dad. I'll be here until the end of my days."

"It's not a bad life sentence."

"I reckon not. Say, I hear you're on the rebound,"

Frank said as if he were discussing the weather and not dropping a bombshell.

"Where did you hear that?" He chuckled. "Who am I rebounding with?"

Then he knew. He remembered Eloise's hand beneath his, the feminine feel of her slender fingers entwined between his. The talk they'd shared on the porch in plain view of anyone walking by. "Cady told you, didn't she?"

"She mentioned seeing you and Eloise together." Frank kept his gaze on the road as if indifferent, but there was no missing his knowing grin.

"We were having a cool drink after fetching the horses. No big deal."

"No big deal. Sure, I get that. Except the two of you were holding hands."

Nothing was private in a small town. Sean chuckled. "Looks are deceiving. Cady saw me comforting a friend, that was all."

"A friend. If that's what you want to call her, fine by me." Uncle Frank's ear-to-ear grin said he knew differently.

He would be wrong. "Eloise has had a tough time. We were talking about it. Friends do that."

"You don't need to convince me."

As if that were even possible. It looked as if his uncle had already made up his mind. Sean shifted on the seat to watch a hawk glide by over the long stretch of field. He and Eloise knew the truth. On the rebound?

He shook his head. It would take a long time before he would be ready to jump in and risk a romantic relationship, rebound or not.

Talk turned to the subjects of the ranch and family until town came into view. The truck rolled to a stop in front of the diner's wide picture windows and a familiar fall of straight golden hair and a cute profile drew his attention. Eloise sat at a booth with a fork poised in midair, listening intently to something her dinner partner said.

Dinner partner. Sean's brain clicked into gear. Her date. She was on a blind date this evening. He frowned at the guy who wore a white dress shirt and dark slacks and had a wholesome, all-American look to him. Sean bristled. He didn't trust that guy. He unlatched his seatbelt, opened the door and dropped to the ground. On the other side of the sun-streaked glass, she turned toward the window, toward him, and her gaze arrowed to his.

Surprise flashed in her gentle green eyes before she returned her attention back to her dinner date. In that one moment he felt dismissed, a friend and not more, just as he'd insisted on being.

Chapter Five

He's coming into the diner! That single realization sent nerves zipping through Eloise's stomach as she watched George cut what remained of his chicken-fried steak into tiny pieces. She trained her eyes on her dinner date but her attention slipped toward the opening door even if her gaze didn't. The door swung open and in the background Sean sauntered in. He planted his hands on his hips but he didn't glance her way. His mile-wide shoulders squared as he ambled down the far aisle with his uncle and out of her field of vision.

"…I am up for a promotion right now," George explained as he precisely set his knife on the edge of his plate. With an unsatisfied frown, he moved it slightly until he was pleased with the angle it made on his plate rim. "You could be looking at the next regional manager."

"Wow." What else could she say to that? It was a plus he actually had a job, but he was really hung up on himself. The signs were hard to miss, blaring like a neon banner throughout the meal.

"There would be a lot of travel involved with being regional manager." He repeated the title, as if simply to hear himself say it. "After that, I could go after the sectional manager position. I have a lot of advancement opportunities, unlike you. That's the problem with thinking small. You have to find a job with room to move."

"Clearly." Yes, that was her problem. She rolled her eyes. She thought too small. Glad she'd met George so she could learn that. She took a bite of grilled chicken and resisted the urge to glance at the clock on the wall behind her. How was it possible that time could move this slowly? Surely the evening was almost over—and the date.

But no, George went right on talking.

"I have a ten-year plan." He precisely speared a perfectly cubed piece of steak with his fork.

"A ten-year plan to be sectional manager?" She tried to listen, she really did, but Sean's magnetism pulled at her attention like he was a black hole sucking up all the gravity in the room. It was his fault, not hers, her gaze slipped just a few inches to the left to bring the farthest booth into her peripheral vision.

Sean. Her hand tingled as she remembered the comfort he'd given her today. She hadn't planned to open up to him or to anyone. She would rather keep the truth behind her breakup with Gerald bottled inside where it was easier to deny. Hearing herself tell part of the story to Sean had helped and she felt better. He'd been easy to talk to.

"No, ten years to realize my plan of being the manager of the entire western half of the country." George chewed exactly twenty-two times before continuing. "I have a deep understanding of paper products and I want to bring that to the world."

"Good for you." She set down her fork, truly able to

say she was no longer hungry. *Lord, please let this date come to an end.*

"Oh, a spill. Here, let me." He scooped up his napkin, reached across the table and dabbed at the base of her water glass. He swiped away the few drops of perspiration that had trickled onto the faded Formica as if it were the Ebola virus needing to be eradicated. He wasn't pleased until he had used a handful of paper napkins from the dispenser to dry off every streak. Once he was satisfied he had decontaminated the site thoroughly, he gave a nod and continued. "I'll be right on schedule if I land the regional position. The key to success is to set short achievable goals that lead you to the end goal."

The waitress must have spotted her distress because she padded over, sneakers squeaking on the tile, and dropped the check on the edge of the table. "Hey, there, Eloise. Do you two need anything else?"

"No, absolutely not," she answered before George could debate the dessert options. It had taken him over twenty minutes to decide on the original meal. The sooner this experience was over, the better. "Thanks, Connie."

She wasn't surprised when George lifted his knife to check his hair in the blade's reflection. He finger-combed a few locks and reached into his pocket.

"You won't mind if we go Dutch, will you?" He tossed her what he probably thought was a charming grin, but it fell far short of the caliber of charm she was used to. He shrugged. "I mean, you understand."

Gladly, she opened her purse and tugged out enough bills to cover her portion and a generous tip. She was just happy the torture was over. "It was interesting meeting you, George."

"So I've been told." He apparently took everything as a compliment. He squinted at the bill, stopped to do the math in his head and reached into his pocket for coins. He left exact change and no tip. He stood and as he watched her do the same, he couldn't quite hide the distaste when his gaze landed on her cane. "Nice meeting you, Eloise."

She clutched her cane's grip, waiting to move until he was safely away from her. From the moment he'd spotted her cane leaning against the window sill, the date had come to a screeching halt. He had only been going through the motions, which she was thankful for because she was definitely not interested in him. But still, it hurt. She wished it didn't, but it did. She was twenty-four years old and she felt passed over and no longer attractive.

Fine, that was vain. The Bible was full of warnings against vanity. But she wanted to feel young and whole and womanly, as she had before the accident, just like any other female her age.

"Whew, dodged a bullet with that one." Connie returned with a pot of coffee in hand. "I saw how pained you looked, so I thought I would give you an out. He looked bored, too."

"Of me, yes, but not when it came to himself," she quipped. Poor George. She hoped he was able to live out his ten-year plan. Everyone deserved a good future. She moved her cane forward and took a step. "Thanks, Connie. I appreciate it more than you know."

"Anytime." Connie went on her way with coffee pot in hand.

"Eloise!" A familiar baritone rang warmly across the diner. Sean studied her over the top of a soda glass. It was hard to say what he might be thinking. His dark blue eyes watched her speculatively as she turned away from the front door and ambled down the aisle. His forehead furrowed. "That date looked painful."

"Yes, thanks for noticing." She stopped at their table, feeling awkward. "Hi, Mr. Granger."

"Hi, Eloise. Haven't seen you around the ranch lately." Frank set his soda glass on the table. "I'm surprised you and Cheyenne aren't out riding. The weather's good for it."

"We have plans later in the week." Another perk about living here again. Horseback rides on lazy summer afternoons had been some of the best parts of her childhood. "I guess that means I'll see you around, Sean."

"I just wanted to make sure you were all right after that experience." He broke off a piece of bread from the basket on the table and swiped butter over it. "It looked as if he wasn't being very nice to you."

"It was a blind date. I wasn't what he was expecting." She shrugged it off. George might not be her idea of a catch, but surely the Lord had made someone just for him. Somewhere there was a woman who cut her steak in precise cubes and chewed exactly twenty-two times and prayed for her soul mate. Eloise liked to think they would find each other. "I can only imagine what my grandmother told his grandmother about me."

"A lot of good things," Sean insisted.

"*Only* the good things," she corrected. "Gran left out everything else, especially the cane."

"Any man who doesn't like your pretty pink cane isn't worthy of you." He spoke up like the friend he had become.

"That's nice. Thanks." Sweetness filled her, which *had* to be gratitude of the highest magnitude and not any other emotion—like interest. "I didn't expect to see you here tonight."

"Wedding stuff. Mrs. G. was whisked away to help view the wedding dress, leaving Uncle Frank and me to fend for ourselves."

"You poor men. Don't either of you know how to cook?"

"Sure, but we didn't want to." He popped a bite of bread into his mouth. His stomach growled, betraying exactly how hungry he was. It would have been expedient to have tossed something on the barbecue. "This way, no dishes. We're smarter than we look."

"So I see." Mirth drew up the corner of her mouth and put little lights into her green irises.

Not that he ought to be noticing. Not that his chest should be tight and achy over seeing her on that date. When the other guy had walked off and left her standing there, relief had hit him in the gut. For a moment he had to wonder if he cared for her more than he wanted to admit, but that couldn't be possible, could it? Ever since his heart was broken, he'd become a lone wolf. A man who needed no one. What he felt for Eloise couldn't be rebound feelings or romantic glimmers or anything like that.

He cleared his throat and washed the bread down with a few gulps of root beer. "Did you want to sit and keep us company?"

"I'd like to, but I can't. My grandmother is expecting me." As if on cue, an electronic tune chimed deep in her bag. She took a step back. "That would be her. She'll want to know how things went with George."

"Will she set you up on another blind date?"

"Heaven knows she will keep at it." Nothing could

hide the love she held for her grandmother, and it was an amazing sight. "Bye!"

"Bye." Sean cleared his throat, doing his best not to watch her walk away. If he had the slightest hook of a grin on his face, his uncle would be sure to notice. More talk of a rebound romance was the last thing he wanted. A man needed his privacy. The door whooshed shut and she was in plain sight through the glass as she ambled to her car.

"Bacon double cheeseburger." The waitress slid the plate on the table in front of him. "And your usual, Frank. I piled on the onion rings. I know how you like them."

"Thank you kindly, Connie." Frank said something else, but the words were lost to Sean as he watched Eloise open her car door.

The wind played with her hair, tossing it across her face. She moved with the grace of a dancer and she shone with the quiet beauty the Bible spoke about. His chest cinched tight, making it hard to breathe. Frank couldn't be right, could he? These feelings he had for her weren't romantic, were they? Was he on the rebound?

No. Sean dismissed the idea and bowed his head as his uncle said the blessing.

Low rays of sunshine slanted through the orchard of fruit trees and onto the rows of the garden patch. New green sprouts speared through the earth to unfurl their stems and leaves. Eloise, changed out of her work clothes and into something more practical for chores, stabbed her cane into the soft grass as she crossed her grandmother's back lawn.

"There's my sweet pea." Edie Tipple looked up from

her weeding. A welcoming smile wreathed her face. "I already got a call from Madge. She said her grandson thought you were real nice."

"He had many good qualities, too." Eloise eased down across from her grandmother. "I'm still not looking to get involved, Gran."

"I mean to change your mind. You never know when the right man will come along." Trouble glinted in her grandmother's green eyes. She tugged at the brim of her hat to keep the sun out of her face. She looked adorable in her pink checkered blouse and pink pants. "I figure on helping you find that right man."

"A woman doesn't need a husband to be happy." As if they hadn't had this conversation before, she plucked at a budding dandelion in the feathery fronds of new carrots, careful not to disturb the growing vegetables. "Look at me. Happy."

"Yes, so I see." Gran didn't sound convinced. "You work all day and spend your evening helping an old lady weed her garden."

"You aren't old to me, Gran, and I like hanging with you, just like I used to when I was little." She plucked a tiny thistle sprout, taking care not to rip the tender roots as she pulled. "Remember when I practically lived here?"

"You, your older sister and I baked every afternoon. Cookies and brownies and pies. Your brothers would eat everything we made." Gran laughed at the good memories they'd shared.

This awesome evening was another great blessing in her life. Time spent with Gran listening to the wind whistle through the grasses and feeling the sunshine on her back made her troubles seem far away. "You don't have to set me up anymore, Gran. I can find my own man when I'm ready."

"I can't seem to help myself." She inched down the row and hunkered over the new section of carrots. Weeds were helpless against her practiced assault. "I can see you didn't fall in love with George. I was hoping he was the one."

"Sadly, no. Not even close." She pulled a buttercup blossom from the feathery greens. The delicate bold yellow petals reminded her of being a little girl running through the fields that would turn yellow with them this time of year. She tucked it behind her ear. "I know that look, Gran. You have someone else in mind."

"I have a backup, it's true. I had you meet the best one first, but this one has prospects, too." Gran glowed with happiness as she worked, considering the possibilities. "His grandmother promises he's a nice boy. He makes up with lots of good traits for what he lacks in other areas."

"Oh, boy." Not again. Eloise laughed. "I don't want to go on another blind date. They're too painful."

"What you need, my girl, is more practice." Gran patted the earth where she'd extracted a particularly long-rooted dandelion. "It's not fair what happened to you. The accident. Spending all that time in a wheelchair—"

"I don't like to think about that time and what I lost," she interrupted. She could only take so much. The year she'd spent as a paraplegic had been the most difficult of her life. "I got through it, but it's over now. I'm looking forward."

"That's wise, dear." Gran swiped her brow and left a faint trace of dust on her forehead. "It was hard rebuilding your life. I watched you do it. You had to leave so much behind. The skating you loved, the man you loved, everything."

"I'm all right." She swallowed hard, refusing to break the cage of denial she'd trapped all her feelings in. "That's what matters. Please don't set me up on another date."

"Too late. I know what's best for you." Gran, as endearing as could be, reached across the row and patted Eloise's hand.

All her life she'd looked up to her grandmother, ran shouting with joy up the front steps to be swept into Gran's hug. The little girl she'd been still could not say no. Gran seemed so big to her, more special than anything on earth.

"I hope you have next Wednesday available." Silver curls fluttered in the wind as she bent over her work. "If not, clear your calendar so you can meet Craig."

"I'm afraid to ask what he does." Eloise pulled a handkerchief from her pocket and shook it out.

"He's a technician at one of those oil-changing places. Now before you think the worst, he's in line for a promotion."

Memories of George flitted into her mind as she gently brushed away the smudge of dirt on her grandmother's forehead. "Goody."

"That's my girl." Pride lit her up. "You'll find your happiness, I promise you that. You can't give up looking, and you can't give up hope."

"I'm not sure I want my happiness to depend on a man." She thought of Gerald and how he hadn't been as stalwart as she'd believed him to be. She would never forget the phone calls she'd made to him and the last messages she'd left on his voice mail. She'd been lonely for him and needed to hear the sound of his voice after a tough day in physical therapy, and what had he been doing? Taking his new skating partner out to an intimate, romantic dinner. She'd been left waiting while his feelings had turned off for her and on for someone else. Almost a year had passed and it still stung.

"When it's the right man, your happiness is assured." Gran sat back on her heels, growing misty remembering. "When your grandfather was alive, my life was perfect. Love made it that way."

"Gramps was great." She couldn't argue. "I'm not sure they make men like him anymore."

"Sure they do. You just have to find him. Your perfect match. The man God means just for you." Gran returned to her weeding, so sure of her view. "Faith, Eloise. You have to believe."

"Of course." Believe? She wanted to. It was a nice idea, but life wasn't that simple and love was painfully complicated. "How about I take a break from believing and start up again, oh, say in five years?"

Gran laughed. "Don't think you are getting out of this date."

"I wouldn't dream of it." She plucked a dandelion and a long-root system out of the soil. A robin flew overhead and landed on the edge of the grass. The bird's head cocked to one side as she listened, then hopped along in search of her supper.

At least her grandmother hadn't yet heard the news that she'd spent time with Sean Granger. That would come one day, but she decided it wouldn't be today. She let the silence lengthen just like the pleasant evening shadows of approaching twilight.

She separated a fragile patch of carrot tops and hunkered down to do some serious weeding. This was her life and she would be content with it.

Chapter Six

H ard to believe a week had gone by without seeing Eloise. Sean gripped the steering wheel as he slowed for a deer in the fields at the side of the road. He kept an eye on her as he approached, ready to stop if she startled and dashed across the road. This time of year, she would have a fawn or two tucked away somewhere so he wanted to take extra care. But she darted safely into the fields so he kept watch for other animals and gave the truck a little more gas.

A whole week. He hadn't been pining for her or anything as dire as that. He'd simply missed out on seeing her. She and Cheyenne had a riding get-together earlier in the week and he figured he might be able to say hi to her then, since he had the expecting mare to check on in the barn. He had intended to ask about the horses they'd rescued. But no, his cousin Tucker had taken possession of the land he'd purchased across the road and had asked for help walking fence lines and making a few minor repairs in the outbuildings. Couldn't say no to the chance to wield a hammer and restring barbed wire, could he? But he'd wondered about her.

There would be no more wondering. He was about

to have the pleasure of her company. He felt as cheerful as the sunlight shining through the windshield. When he hit town, he hung a right and followed the detour on Second Street to avoid the vendors setting up for the town's yearly summer festival. The few miles he had to go seemed like ten. Maybe he was looking forward to seeing Eloise more than he'd thought.

Anticipation buzzed through him as he turned off into the paved lane that rolled through fields, trees and blooming flowers to the Lark Song Inn. When Uncle Frank had called him into the barn with a message to meet Eloise with the horse trailer, he'd had to hide the gladness sweeping through him. He didn't want his uncle to misread things. He didn't bother to hide it now.

Eloise was nice. Who wouldn't enjoy spending time with her? Add to that the fact she was a casualty of romance too, how could he resist wanting to see her? It was a comfort to have a buddy going through the same thing he was. Even a lone wolf needed a buddy.

He parked, grabbed the keys and hopped into the pleasantly warm morning. The parking lot only had a few cars. A middle-aged couple led the way down the porch while a hotel employee carted their luggage after them.

"Good morning." He stepped out of the way to let them down the stairs first. They returned the greeting, quite relaxed and content. That's when he caught sight of Eloise. Wow, she took his breath away. She breezed through the doorway wearing a pink T-shirt, boot-cut jeans and riding boots. She'd obviously changed out of her work clothes for their next horse-hunting adventure.

"Sean. You made record time." She waved the gray

Stetson she carried in her free hand and plopped it on
her head as she crossed the porch. "You had to be standing right beside Mr. Granger when I gave him the message."

"No, but he didn't waste time getting a hold of me."
He didn't add that his uncle was hoping a romance
would develop. Frank was definitely going to be dis-
appointed on that score. Sean waited while she tapped
down the steps. "You didn't waste any time finding
more horses."

"Actually they found me, or the humane society did.
I had spoken to them last week, of course." She joined
him on the pathway and they backtracked to the truck.
"I—"

"Eloise!" A child's voice rang in the air behind them.
Cady's little goddaughter Julianna waved at them, all
dressed in purple. "Daddy said I could come, okay?"

She pounded down the stairs in her glittery grape
sneakers. Too late to say no to her now. He lifted a brow
to Eloise in a silent comment.

"Do you mind?" She bit her bottom lip, maybe worried he might get mad.

"How could I? First I was spending the morning
with one pretty gal, now I get to spend it with two."
He opened the truck door for her, noticing she smelled
faintly like honeysuckle.

"You are a gentleman, Sean Granger."

"I try."

Threads of pure blue sparkles wove through the emerald depths of her irises. He'd never seen a more arresting color. She was wholesome femininity and sunny
beauty and he wasn't sure why his chest cinched up so
hard he couldn't breathe. Probably any man would have
the same reaction to her. It wasn't romantic feelings he

felt. Probably gratitude for a friendship that was obviously cementing.

That had to be it. Satisfied with his conclusion, he waited for Julianna to skip across the lot, caught her elbow to help her up into the cab first and turned to Eloise. He knew the touch of her hand and the slender fit of her fingers against his.

Nice. This is friendship, he insisted as his heart skipped a single beat—just one. Nothing to worry about. Once she was helping Julianna with her seatbelt, he shut the door and circled the truck to the driver's side.

"Now that I've joined the team," he said as he started the engine. "What are the details? Where do we go?"

"We take a left at the county road and keep on driving for ten miles." Eloise pulled a pink memo out of her jeans pocket. Glossy gold hair curtained her face, leaving only the tip of her nose and the dainty cut of her chin visible. "Angie from the humane society is already on site. She says there are four horses and that's all I know."

"Abused or just unwanted, like the last pair?" He nosed the truck down the lane.

"I don't know." She folded the paper back up into quarters. "They are doing the assessments right now."

"So you don't know if these will have the temperament you're looking for?"

"They are in need. Cady says that's more important."

Julianna nodded. "They need love," she chimed in, as cute as a button.

He remembered when his little sister, Giselle, was that age. Although she was grown up and in college now, she was still as sweet to him. He shared a smile over the top of Julianna's head and the silent connection he felt with Eloise defied words.

Checking for traffic, he saw the road was completely clear and turned left. Fields spread out as far as the eye could see, broken only by trees, a few houses scattered far and wide and the occasional herds of grazing cattle and horses. "How are Hershey and Licorice?"

"Licorice gives kisses," Julianna answered, as serious as a judge. "Hershey likes apples the best."

Not exactly the information he was after and across the cab Eloise's gaze found his again. It was a shared moment where words weren't needed. It was nice to have a real friend, one he was in tune with.

"After they had a good bath and brush down, the farrier came by to tend to their hooves and shoes." She fingered the edge of the paper she held. "They are sweet guys. Licorice seems relieved to have so much attention again. He's already making friends with everyone. Hershey is having a harder time."

"He stares down the aisle all day," Julianna explained. "He's got sad eyes."

"He's grieving. He's especially tender-hearted and he's taken all these changes very hard." She'd spent the bulk of her breaks and lunch hour making friends with him. "We are all trying to comfort him. Everyone already loves both horses."

"I'm sure they aren't being spoiled."

"Not at all." Her day felt brighter. It couldn't be because of Sean, right? She leaned back in the seat and savored the fall of sun on her face and the sense of freedom at being temporarily released from her managerial duties. "I'm certainly not guilty of that, right, Julianna?"

"Right." The girl shook her head emphatically and her twin braids bounced. "Me neither."

Sean chuckled. Eloise felt comfortable in his presence. Not at all like Friday night when it had been a struggle to make conversation with George. "I was going to saddle them up and give them a test ride this afternoon and could use some help. Are you interested?"

"I'm game. Count me in." He squared his impressive shoulders. He had come when she'd asked, and she thought about that, finding one more thing among the many to like about the man.

"Can I come, too?" Julianna steepled her hands as if in prayer. "Please, please please?"

"After we find out how they handle, then you can see what your dad says." Eloise gave one braid a gentle tug, knowing that would make the girl smile.

"Bummer. I know how to ride, you know. Aunt Cady lets me ride her horse." Sparkles glittered in her eyes full of excitement and childhood wonder. "I love horses, too. I've asked Dad one hundred times and he still says I can't have one. We live in the city."

"Yes, there's no place for a horse in a brownstone." Eloise understood the girl's love of horses. It was a phase she hadn't ever fully outgrown. Her mare, Pixie, lived in her grandmother's field, as she had for the last fourteen years. "I got my horse when I was your age."

"You did? Cool." Julianna sighed. "I know you aren't supposed to pray for yourself. That's not the right way to pray. You are supposed to think of others and pray for them. That's what Dad says. So, do you know what?"

"What?"

"I pray for my horse. She's somewhere and I want her to be happy. Maybe that way she can find me. And if she does, maybe she can be gold with a white mane."

Julianna's forehead puckered with concern. "Do you think that's being selfish like my mom?"

On the other side of the truck, Sean caught her eye. He drove with both hands on the wheel and kept most of his attention on the road, but in the brief moment their gazes met an unspoken understanding passed between them. Probably because they were on the same wavelength.

Julianna's mother had left the family for a richer man. She couldn't imagine how much that would hurt a little girl. Eloise cleared the emotion from her throat. Her parents' marriage was rock solid. Her grandparents on both sides had been the same. "No, I don't think it's selfish. You are asking for the horse to be happy first, even if you never get to meet her, right?"

"Right." Julianna sighed. "But I hope I do."

"Me, too." She liked to think there was a very lucky and nice horse out there wanting a little girl to love. She let her eyes drift shut. *Please, Lord, if it's possible, give Julianna her dream.*

"I saw that," Sean said after she'd opened her eyes. "I know what you asked for."

"How?"

"Because I did, too."

It was tough not to like him even more for that. It was a good thing she spotted the road they needed to turn on to so that she didn't need to analyze it. There were horses to rescue. "Take a right there by the pine trees."

"Sure thing."

The truck hit the dirt lane with a bump. They bounced down the wide private road lined by thick trees and she unfolded her memo to make sure she remembered the directions correctly. "We're looking for a mailbox with the last name Noon. It should be on the left-hand side."

"I see it." He slowed the truck to make the turn. The driveway was in terrible shape, overgrown as if no vehicle had passed there for some time. Fresh tracks through grass, weeds and a sprouting blackberry bush testified it was an actual driveway.

"No worries." Sean gave the wheel a slow spin. "I've got four-wheel drive."

"Let's hope you don't need it." She couldn't imagine getting the horses and trailers out if they did. Julianna seemed to enjoy the jolting and pitching, her eyes shining with the importance of their adventure.

It wasn't long before a clearing gave way to a mass of parked vehicles and the saddest sight. Eloise gasped aloud at the four shapes huddled in the shade of a maple tree in a barren, tumbling-down corral. The shapes were animals covered with thick layers of dried-on mud and dirt.

The sharp hint of bones pierced the horses' sides. Her vision blurred with hot, shocked tears and obscured the image of the half-starved horses. Sean's truck rolled to a stop and she wondered if she should make Julianna stay in the cab or call her father to inform him the situation might be too graphic for her.

But it was too late. Julianna unclicked her belt, rising to her knees on the seat. She gripped the steering wheel, straining to look. "What happened to them? Why are they like that?"

"They're starving, sweetie." Sean answered, his baritone layered with sadness. "Someone left them to fend for themselves."

The place was obviously abandoned. The old farmhouse stood dark and silent with weeds growing on the walkway and obscuring the front steps.

"It's been foreclosed on. When the appraiser came to take a look at the property for the bank, she found this." A woman who must be Angie, the lady from the county shelter, strode over in a simple shirt, jeans and boots. "Nate is taking a look at them right now. They seem glad to see us, poor things."

"It's good to meet you, Angie." Eloise didn't remember tumbling from the truck, only that she was on the ground staring at the horses. She swiped at her eyes. "I'm sorry, I wasn't prepared for this. Julianna?"

"I've got her," Sean answered. The girl's hand was tucked safely in his as they watched Nate work with the animals.

"We're going to help them, right?" Tears rolled down the girl's face.

"That's why we're here." Sean was ten feet tall in her view. Shoulders square, spine straight, unfailingly decent. It was really hard not to look at him and think, "amazing."

"I'm sorry to bring you all the way out here like this." Angie glanced at her cell screen before tucking it into her pocket. "I was just getting ready to call you. It's worse than I thought. I suppose you are rethinking your offer?"

"Not at all." The wind puffed lazily against her as she turned toward the fence. One of the horses lifted her head over the top rail, nostrils scenting the air, chocolate eyes gleaming with the smallest hope. "My boss would not want me to walk away from this."

"Whew. I can't tell you how glad I am to hear that." Angie tugged at her hat brim. "Our donations are down in this economy, and we are stretched thin as it is. I'm not sure we have the resources for this, even with Nate donating his services. They are good horses, as far as I can tell. Calm. A little skittish, but that's to be expected."

"How long have they been like this?"

"Probably a few months. I talked to a neighbor. No one realized the animals were left behind or they would have done something sooner. The folks who left probably had no money to deal with the animals, but they should have called us. We could have helped. That's why we're here."

A sad situation. Eloise set the tip of her cane on the uneven ground. "At least we can help now. How long before we can trailer them?"

"As soon as Nate is done. I think he intends to follow you back to town. They are going to need some special care."

"We will make sure they get it." Determined, she joined Sean and Julianna at the fence. The horse had poked her head through the wood rungs and buried her rather substantial-size face against Julianna's stomach and chest. The mare leaned into the little girl with obvious need.

"She likes me," Julianna breathed, holding on tightly to the animal so dirty it was hard to make out her original color. "I like her, too."

"So I see. You are friends already." She laid the palm of her hand against the horse's sun-warmed neck, hoping the animal could feel in her touch that everything was going to be all right.

"I'm going to help the vet." Sean reached over to brush a strand of hair from her eyes. The stroke of his fingertips was brief but tender. Her breath caught, but he didn't seem affected. Calm and collected, he moved away, his gait confident and easy, his movements athletic and sure. He ducked between the rails and paused to reassure the horses before he moved a step closer.

Maybe it was her imagination, but the sunshine seemed to brighten all around him.

"I feel sorry for Julianna's dad." Eloise swung up on her good leg and settled into the saddle. She patted Licorice's neck and tightened the reins to keep him from sidestepping. "The girl refused to leave Dusty's side."

Julianna had named the mare because she was so dusty. The two had bonded and as soon as they'd arrived back at the inn, the horse lumbered down the ramp and ran straight to the child. They were inseparable. Fortunately, the chef had sent a picnic lunch out to the stable for everyone working on the new arrivals, so the girl had gotten lunch.

Eloise reined Licorice around. "I don't know how Adam is going to get Julianna back home to New York."

"I overheard him saying the same thing." Sean eased into his saddle, although Hershey wasn't too sure about a new rider. The big bay gelding danced in place but didn't discourage the seasoned rider who commanded him with a gentle hand and reassured him in low tones. "I think it was love at first sight."

"You are definitely right." She tugged the brim of her hat lower to cut the sun's glare. "That is the most dangerous kind of horse love. I don't recommend it as I'm still in the midst of it."

"Me, too. It's one love that has no end." He felt the gelding's hesitancy. The animal kept looking around, searching for someone long gone. He laid his hand on the gelding's neck, so the horse could feel the comfort of his touch. "You did nothing wrong, buddy. Are you going to be all right?"

The horse's sigh was answer enough. He plodded along but his feelings didn't seem to be into it. Poor fellow. Larks twittered on branches and jays squawked from the fence line as he guided the horse down the sidewalk, trailing Eloise. She sat straight and tall in her saddle, graceful as always and her long hair trailed in the wind.

"Where should we go?" she asked over her shoulder.

He pressed his heels lightly to bring Hershey alongside the other horse. "Do you know what sounds good after that lunch we had?"

"An ice-cream cone?"

"How did you know?"

"A wild guess."

"Proof great minds think alike." Of all the ways he'd seen Eloise, and he'd liked every one, this had to be his favorite view of her. Astride a horse, she was carefree and relaxed, girl-next-door wholesome and unguarded. On the back of the horse, she seemed less restrained, less careful. Maybe it was because she didn't need her cane to move through the world. She dazzled in a modest, genuine way he could not describe with words but could feel with his soul.

"I'm sorry to tell you this, Sean, but a great mind? You? I don't think so." Humor crinkled attractively in the corners of her eyes.

"Ouch. That's hard on a man's ego."

"I would think your ego would be used to it by now." Dimples bracketed the demure curve of her mouth. "If it's any consolation, my mind isn't great either. Just so-so."

"I'm mostly so-so," he quipped. "Just ask my brother. He's a decorated Army Ranger and I'm the never-do-well in the family."

"The black sheep?"

"Baaah." So, he liked to make her laugh. Nothing else felt important right now, just that she was happy. The geldings pranced quickly down the lane and onto the shoulder of the county road. No traffic buzzed by, but when a vehicle did it would be a good way to judge how steady the horses were. "How about you? Let me guess, you are the perfect daughter."

"Me? No way. That's my older sister. Gabby is perfect. She was the A student, I was the B student. She has her own design business in Jackson—she was hired to do the inn, that's how I met Cady. I'm the slacker living with my parents."

"You still live at home?"

"Guilty as charged."

"Honestly? I did, too. I came back after college. Now I live with Uncle Frank and my cousins. Although it will be one less cousin in a few weeks. Autumn is moving out after the wedding." He pressed Hershey into a trot. "We have a lot in common, Eloise."

"I know, it's scary." She urged her mount to keep up with him. "Very scary."

"I have a question for you." He nudged Hershey into a smooth canter. Steel shoes rang on the pavement in harmony as they ran along. "You haven't heard from that blind-date guy again, have you?"

"Me? Oh, no. George was never interested in me." She glanced over her shoulder. "We're in luck. A hay truck is coming up on us."

He hadn't noticed the rumble of the diesel engine closing in. All he could see was Eloise lighting up the world around him. He shook his head, bringing the landscape into focus. The blue sky, green grass fields and the first glimpse of town up ahead seemed distantly dull next to her. The semi's engine whined as it downshifted. "I guess we'll see how the horses take a little distraction."

"My guess is nice and steady. Licorice handles like a dream." Affection and pride for the horse softened her and she'd never looked more awe-inspiring than when she leaned forward to pat the gelding's neck. "Isn't that right, boy?"

The truck rolled by and Sean didn't notice the hit of the back draft or the tiny bits of hay raining down from the load. All he could see was Eloise's tender compassion as she spoke to the horse and her caring spirit as she urged Licorice into a gallop, leaving him and Hershey behind in their dust.

Chapter Seven

❧

"Licorice is really fast." Eloise turned in her saddle. "I wanted to push him and see what he had. Wow."

"Impressive." Sean pulled a winded Hershey into a slow walk. "Like he's part Thoroughbred."

"He's a great horse." She watched the gelding's ears flicker, taking in every word. His neck arched with a touch of pride and his luxurious black mane rippled in the warm breeze. "My guess is he was ridden often. Someone spent a lot of time with him."

"That would explain a lot." He rocked along with the horse's gait. He appeared powerful in the saddle, utterly Western and heroic as if he could right wrongs and fight outlaws into submission.

Eloise shook her head to scatter her thoughts. Highly inappropriate. He was a friend, nothing more. A very handsome friend. Muscles shaped the cut of his T-shirt. He was in incredible shape, but his power was more than physical, it went deeper as if straight to the soul.

"Hershey keeps glancing back like he's expecting someone to materialize and his life can go back to the way it was." Sympathy etched into the hard rugged lines of Sean's face. "He wants to go back in time, and I can't do that for him."

The man was way too gorgeous for his good and for hers. She drew in a deep breath. Time to stop noticing these things. She looked up to realize they were at the drive-in. How did they get there? She had no idea because she'd been watching Sean and not the scenery.

She guided Licorice into the driveway and straight toward the drive-thru lane.

"I can empathize." She drew her horse to a stop in the shade of the building and studied the lighted display. "I remember lying in the hospital staring up at the ceiling tiles and asking God to take me back in time so I could change the events of that evening. I wanted back what I'd lost."

"You knew you couldn't skate again that soon?" Sean sidled up beside her, forehead furrowed with concern, sitting tall and straight. If a girl were to lay her cheek against his wide shoulder, she would feel safe and incredibly protected.

Not that she was that girl. She steeled her spine. "Oh, yes. As soon as they looked at the X-rays, they told me I'd never return to the ice."

Sean opened his mouth to say something, probably to ask the obvious question but thankfully the speaker squawked to life. Licorice stood calmly at the noise. Hershey danced a few nervous steps and then settled.

"Welcome to the Steer In." A cheerful teenage girl's voice popped and cracked over the ancient system. "Is that you, Eloise?"

"Hi, Chloe. How are you doing today?"

"It's a quiet afternoon, so good. What can I get you?"

"A soft chocolate ice-cream cone." She shivered when Sean leaned close.

"A strawberry for me," he rumbled in low, smoky tones.

"Oh, is this like a date?" Chloe blurted over the speaker loud enough to carry to the nearby car parked beneath the awning. Two gray-haired ladies glanced their way, familiar smiles flashing as they turned to watch the proceedings. They were, as luck would have it, friends of Gran's.

It was too much to hope she wouldn't be recognized. Impossible, really, since the women in the car had known her since birth.

"Not a date." She was quick to correct loud enough for her voice to carry. "Don't say things like that, Chloe. You're going to ruin any chance I have of my grandmother abandoning her plans to marry me off."

"Sorry," Chloe laughed.

"You wouldn't happen to know those ladies over there?" Sean leaned in and splayed his palm on the saddle's pommel. "They're waving."

"I know them." All too well. Mrs. Parnell was Gran's oldest friend. Mrs. Plum was Gran's second-oldest friend. They lunched together at least once a week after their church meeting.

No way was she going to keep this private. Her grandmother was sure to find out. As she touched her heels to Licorice's sides and he obligingly stepped forward, she fought off a wave of panic. All Gran had to do was to talk to Frank Granger, and how hard would it be for the two of them to make Sean feel obligated to take her to dinner? Putting him in that uncomfortable position was the last thing she wanted.

"It's my treat." He leaned across her to hand money to Chloe at the window. "Keep the change."

It was too late to protest. Chloe darted away before Eloise could dig out the fold of dollar bills she'd hidden in her jeans pocket.

"The horses are handling all of this just fine, don't you think?" Sean knuckled back his hat, revealing more of his face. His blue eyes resonated the manly kindness she'd come to expect. A girl could lose herself dreaming about him.

But not her. She was thankful for that. She cleared her throat, surprised her voice sounded thin and scratchy when she answered. "Yes, I do. Hershey will be calmer once he gets used to all the changes he's facing."

"He needs time. That's all." Sitting in the saddle, backlit by the brilliant blue sky and the sun-kissed greenery of grass and trees, he was a compelling sight.

Not that she was compelled.

"He might require a bit of work. I'll volunteer to train him, if there's a need."

"Thanks." Her voice sounded squeaky. "I'll keep that in mind."

Chloe popped into view through the take-out window and produced two cones. Eloise handed one over to Sean along with a few paper napkins Chloe also dispensed.

"Have fun!" The teenager called out. Clearly she had high hopes for their "date."

The horses plodded forward lazily. It was a perfect summer afternoon. Not too hot, but hot enough to make the ice cream taste like an icy luxury. Not too windy, just a light puff of air stirring up the scents of earth and grass and horse. The noise from the main street increased as they circled the lot to the exit lane. Colorful booths and awnings stretched as far as the eye could see up the street. A red banner strung from light poles read, "Welcome to Wild Horse, Wyoming's Pioneer Days Festival."

"When do you have to be back to work?" he asked.

"Cady said not to hurry." She leaned back in her saddle, tilting her face toward his. "Are you thinking what I'm thinking?"

"That's an affirmative." He gave his ice-cream cone a taste and let the strawberry sweetness melt on his tongue. "Nothing like hitting the festival on the first day. We'll get the best view of stuff and it's not crowded."

"Yes. Wait until tonight." She gave her cone a twirl, neatly catching all the drips. "I hadn't realized how much I've missed all this. I got caught up chasing after things that didn't last, at least not for me. Now that I'm home, I've forgotten how special this all is."

"Small-town festivals?"

"Yes, and small-town life." She sighed as the horses plodded leisurely down the empty section of the street. "Before I was always so busy and focused. When I was on the ice, I had to shut out everything else. There was only practice."

"And the falls? That ice looks like a hard place to land." He had to quip; it was who he was. It was easier to joke than ask harder questions.

"I don't miss the falls." She had a wonderful laugh, reserved and whimsical. "But I miss the skating. I trained and I trained. It took me an extra two years to squeak in college courses so I could get a degree. Between skating and school, I didn't do a whole lot of living. I put off everything. Fun weekends, vacations, seeing movies and even the idea of marriage and a family."

"Are you second-guessing the choices you made?" He knew how that could be.

"No. I can't imagine following any other dream. It simply hurt when it ended." She looked wistful and not bitter, retrospective and not sad. "If the accident hadn't happened, I would still be skating."

"What was your favorite part?" He took a big bite of ice cream and let it melt in his mouth, watching as she licked a dab of chocolate ice cream off her bottom lip. She was as sweet as could be, trying to eat her cone before it dripped all over her.

His chest warmed with new emotions, which had to be admiration and respect—certainly nothing romantic. He was a lone wolf. Lone wolves didn't do romance.

"The competitions were way too stressful to be my favorite part. The travel was tough because we were focused on our training and our performances." She frowned in concentration and gave her melting cone another lick. "It was the day-to-day skating I loved. Being on the ice when it was just me soaring. I felt like I did when I was little skating on Gran's winter pond. It's all I ever wanted to do."

"You didn't only lose a vocation, but a calling. Something you loved."

"Yes." She turned those incredible, honest eyes at him. "But there are worse things to lose in life. How about you? What have you lost?"

"My older brother a few years back." He bit into the sugary cone, crunching as he gathered the courage to let down his guard. "Tim was an Army Ranger killed in action."

"I'm so sorry."

"Me, too. It was a hard blow for everyone in my family."

"How did you handle it?"

"Mostly, I felt lost. Drifting. As if everything I'd thought about myself and about life changed."

"Trauma will do that to you." Empathy layered her words.

"The earth had been knocked out from beneath me and I no longer wanted the same things I once did." The first vendor's booth was close, so he eased Hershey to a stop. "One loss made everything shift. I couldn't see life the same way. My brother wasn't in it. I knew the phone would never ring with him on the other end of the line. I no longer believed only good things happened."

"Life can change in an instant. I learned that lesson, too." She daintily bit into the rim of her cone. "It makes you appreciate each day more, I think. Here and right now it is such a beautiful afternoon. I want to soak it in, every detail, and remember it always."

"Even me?" He finished off his cone.

"Especially you." She blushed a little, but when he nodded in understanding, she relaxed. They were on the same wavelength, they didn't even need the words. She'd never experienced it with anyone else before. "We can tether the horses here in the shade."

"And bring them some water from the hot-dog vendor." He gestured with a nod at the nearby booth before dismounting in a single powerful movement. His boots hit the ground with a muffled thud.

"Good idea." She managed not to spill her cone as she swung her leg over and eased to the pavement. "We'll keep an eye on them for a bit. Make sure they don't start worrying about being left again."

"Hershey's already looking nervous. It's okay, boy." He stroked the gelding's nose in slow, gentle glides that made the horse calm.

The moment she let go of the saddle horn she realized her mistake. Too late to get back on the horse without having to explain to Sean. She kept her weight on her good leg and leaned lightly on Licorice for support. For a little while, she'd forgotten about what the doctors had labeled a disability. She had been free from her partial paralysis and the cane she relied on.

"Did you forget something?" Sean ambled closer and tugged her hat brim up a few inches so he could study her face.

"I didn't forget it. I just didn't bring it." Her cane was leaning against the stable wall, right where she'd left it. Self-conscious, she wanted nothing more than to get back on that horse where she didn't have to be less than. On the back of a horse, she could be like any other young woman. That's the way she wanted Sean to see her.

"No problem." He held out his arm. "You can lean on me."

"No, I would be embarrassed." Every step she would take would remind her of how different she was. It would remind her even more strongly of the woman she no longer was.

"What's to be embarrassed about?" He appeared genuinely confused, as if he couldn't begin to see any problems. Proof of the kind of man he was. He caught her arm in his, sun-warmed and substantial. "Don't worry. I won't let you fall."

"I didn't think you would." She took a step with her weak leg, hating the weight she transferred onto Sean's forearm. "I weigh too much."

"You weigh the perfect amount. You don't have to worry, Eloise." He took a step forward to show her he was better than any cane she'd ever used. "I don't notice your limp. When I look, I see you."

"You must need glasses." She had to tease so he couldn't guess what his words meant to her. She would never forget the look on Gerald's face when he saw her sitting in a wheelchair for the first time. It was a blend of horror and pity that was burned on her brain, although he had quickly covered it up well enough. "I could recommend a good eye doctor."

"There's nothing wrong with my vision."

Before she could argue teasingly, the rest of her ice cream was plucked out of her hand. She turned, surprised to see Licorice crunching away on the last of the sugar cone.

Sean burst into laughter. "Next time we'll have to get some for the horses."

"I hope that doesn't give him a stomachache." Good humor chased away her worries. Life was good as she and Sean headed down the street together.

It was easy being with Eloise. Sean tucked his wallet into his back pocket and handed over the twenty. The vendor looked pleased as punch as she accepted it and began to wrap up the sale.

"The wind chimes are lovely, but it's too much." Eloise folded a strand of blond hair behind her ear in a shy gesture that only proved how cute she was.

Cute. He kept using that word for her over and over again. It wasn't the only word. Awesome came to mind. So did endearing. Beautiful was another that described her in any situation. To think she was self-conscious about her injury. Her limp was invisible, her loveliness outshone it tenfold.

"It will be something to remember today by. Something good, after the rough morning we all had." The neglected horses stayed at the back of his mind. He knew they were at the back of hers, too. The set of halters and leads she'd bought from one of the other vendors was testimony enough they were not far from her mind. At least the animals were more comfortable now. He accepted the bag from the sales lady and added it to the bundle he carried. "Whenever the wind blows, you can think of me."

"Because you're a bunch of hot air?"

"Ha ha." He bit his lip to keep from laughing. Before he could come up with a snazzy comeback, he heard someone say her name.

"Eloise, is that you?" a fragile voice warbled. A delicate elderly lady padded up to lay her hand on Eloise's arm. "Where is your cane, sweet pea? How are you getting around?"

"Gran." Eloise's jaw dropped. As if mortified, she sputtered for a second unable to think of what to say.

Sure, he knew how it looked with her hand tucked lightly on his forearm and with him carrying all her purchases. He cleared his throat. "I'm squiring her around this afternoon. Mrs. Tipple, we met a long time ago when I was a teenager."

"I remember. You were trouble, if I recall. Couldn't stop fidgeting during the candlelight service." She smiled, a timeless beauty. "You are one of the Granger boys."

"Guilty. I hope you don't mind I've stolen your granddaughter for the afternoon."

"Not at all." She chirped with happiness. "You aren't married, I take it?"

"No, but I'm not looking to be." He broke the news gently as Eloise gave her grandmother a hug.

"We're just friends, Gran, so don't get any ideas. Promise me?" Unmistakable love made her luminous. "I'm going out to dinner with Craig, but that is the last fix-up. No more."

"Take pity on her, Mrs. Tipple." Sean couldn't resist helping her cause. He liked Eloise. He'd do about anything for her. "I know how she feels. It's humiliating every time a new date doesn't work out."

"Why, I never thought of it that way before." The older lady furrowed her brow, adorably puzzled. "I can't think of why that would be."

"Gran, you found your perfect match on the first try. That's a great gift few of us are blessed with." She probably looked a lot like her grandmother did fifty years ago, Sean decided. She had the same willowy build and oval face and eyes shining like flawless emeralds. There was strength, too, the kind that went all the way to the soul.

"I'd best leave you kids to your fun." A grandmother's love beamed from her as she gave Eloise one final pat. "Don't think you have to hurry over tonight. I've got all the weeding done except for the tomatoes."

"Don't you dare do it without me." Eloise's warning held no bite, only sweetness. "See you later."

Her fingertips settled on his arm as she turned to watch her grandmother join her friends at a nearby booth. He laughed. "I finally have it figured out, chickie."

"What, exactly?" She sparkled as she leaned lightly on his arm.

"You spend a lot of evenings with your grandmother. You live with your parents." He heard his phone ring and pulled it out of his pocket. "I'm starting to see the real you."

"Oh, no. You don't want to be associated with someone so drab. Or would dull be a better word?"

"You? Dull? That's impossible." The experience of holding her on his arm had brought him closer to her than he'd expected, both physically and emotionally. Because she'd left her cane behind he had been near enough to see the twinkle lighting her eyes when she'd spotted the wind chimes for the first time.

Eloise was quietly exhilarating and she was easy to be with. There was no knot of anxiety in his chest. Meryl had always tied him up in knots, leaving him to wonder if he'd done things right or wrong. Being with Eloise was as natural as breathing. He stepped out of the flow of pedestrian traffic. "Is that your phone?"

"Probably. If not, then it's my guilt calling. I'm having too much fun. I should be on my way to work." She tugged out her cell and checked it.

"I heard Cady say not to rush back. No guilt necessary." He liked that about her, though. She was conscientious.

"Cady sent a text. She wants me to stop by the feed store and pick up a few things for the new horses."

"Let me see." He leaned close. His cheek brushed hers as he scanned the list. Her skin felt satin soft and he breathed in another hint of honeysuckle. It was nice. He kept using that word, but it was the truth. Being with her was so enjoyable, he wouldn't want to be anywhere else.

He focused on the list typed across the phone's little screen. "It's all easy stuff to tie on the saddles. It's doable."

"Definitely." She didn't move away.

Neither did he. The breeze danced through her hair, sending a stray wisp against his jaw. "The feed store is across the street from the horses. It couldn't be an easier errand."

"True."

Time stood still. The noise and heat and scents from the nearby hot-dog vendor became background to the slow, drum-like thud of his heart. He leaned in, so close their noses almost bumped. Her soft mouth opened slightly, betraying her surprise. The same surprise tapped like mad through his veins, but he couldn't seem to jerk away and put proper space between them. All he could see was her. Her big soulful eyes, her incredibly beautiful face, her lips. She was sugar-cookie sweet. He wanted to kiss her tenderly to match the tender adoration filling him.

Adoration? He furrowed his brow. That wasn't what he wanted to feel. What he wanted was to be unattached, a male wolf prowling the wilderness on his own answering to no one. So why was he inching closer?

Don't do it, he told himself. Kissing her wouldn't be right. It wouldn't be fair.

It was all he wanted.

Chapter Eight

"No." Her slim hand shot out and splayed across his sternum. "Sean, what are you doing?"

He swallowed. Good question. He was obviously being stupid.

Except it didn't feel stupid. It felt right to care for her. He shrugged. "I'm a man. Do we ever really know what we're doing?"

The quip worked. The tension taut in her shoulders relaxed a smidgeon. The stress tightening her jaw eased. Confusion continued to cloud her eyes as she stood like an island in the moving stream of the crowd, and he had to make that right. He hated to think he'd hurt her or caused her turmoil of any kind.

"Proof there really is something wrong with men." Her puzzlement turned to a chuckle.

"True. We're deeply flawed. Forgive me."

"I'll think about it." She tilted her head to one side, considering him. She held out one hand, since she couldn't take a decent step without him. "I think you have had too much fun, mister."

"Guilty. I have a weakness for street fairs. I lose all common sense." His arm linked with hers, offering her his strength and his friendship as if the moment had never happened. "Let's stop and get water for the horses before we hit the feed store."

"It's a plan." She pasted on what she hoped was a smile, one that wasn't too bright and yet neatly hid the knot of confusion and disappointment tangled inside her.

They said nothing more, just little necessary things, as Sean ordered two big cups of water and they took them back to Licorice and Hershey. He tried to hide it, but she noticed the tension bunched along his square-cut jaw and the crinkles etched into the corners of his eyes. The friendship between them was strained. The easy camaraderie vanished. Sean had crossed a line she hadn't been comfortable with and she didn't know how to repair it.

He probably hadn't been thinking, just like he'd said. Maybe he was lonely, too. Maybe for a moment he'd felt less so and that's why he'd moved in to kiss her. She was convenient, she acknowledged silently as she held the cup for Licorice. Sean couldn't possibly have actually meant that kiss.

Sadness eked into her, and she gripped the side of the hitching post to balance her weight. Why did that make her so sad? As the horse lipped and slurped, she watched Sean out of the corner of her eye. He stood stoic in front of Hershey, holding the cup of water at an angle.

"If you want to hand me your phone, I'll run across the street and pick up the stuff." His words were nearly monotonous with strain as he held out his hand, wide palm up. Apology shadowed his gaze and she looked away.

She fished her phone from her pocket and handed it

over. But as he strode away without a word, dependable shoulders straight, gait athletic, an impressive man of good character, she felt her heart tug.

If only her gaze didn't follow him across the street. When he strode through the door and out of her sight, it was as if the sun dimmed.

Don't start feeling for him, she warned. No matter what she could not start to wonder what would have happened if they had kissed. She would be foolish to start wanting what she could not have.

Dumb. That's how he felt, like the biggest doofus in the county. Sean dismounted swiftly as soon as they reached the shadow of the inn's stables to fetch Eloise's cane. It was right where she'd left it, propped against the wall in the breezeway outside Licorice's stall. He seized the handle and hurried back just as she was dismounting.

"Thanks." She broke the silence, which had haunted them on the ride back.

He didn't know what to say after nearly kissing her. He couldn't bring up the subject again because it would only make those unhappy lines etch into her face. He didn't want that. Mom always said, "Less said, soonest mended," so he decided to go with the age-old adage, but he remained troubled. He'd hurt their friendship over an almost-kiss she hadn't wanted.

He had.

Clearly his feelings were bigger than he wanted to admit, even to himself. It was a lonely place to be. Disappointment crept around him like talons, digging deep. He prayed it didn't show as he took Licorice by the bit.

"I'll walk them in to Rocco. He's the one in charge of the horses?"

"Yes. I'll come with you. I want to see how the new additions are doing." She kept her gaze on the uneven gravel path ahead of her, as if that required her concentration.

He wasn't fooled. She did very well with her impaired walk. She didn't need to put so much concentration into it. She wanted to, and he didn't blame her.

He'd acted on feelings, not on thought. Maybe Uncle Frank was right. Maybe he was rebounding and he didn't even mean to be. Rebounding was not his style. He had decided to be a loner. He wanted no connections to any woman. That was the best way to heal from a broken relationship instead of jumping feetfirst into a new one.

Something tugged on his shirtsleeve. Sad-eyed Hershey lifted his horsy eyebrows in a show of sympathy.

"You're a good guy, Hersh." He patted the horse's nose.

The gelding nickered low in his throat, as if in perfect agreement.

"Eloise!" A child's voice echoed in the rafters above, accompanied by the patter of running feet. Julianna charged around the corner like a cute, purple butterfly. "You gotta come see! I have Dusty's stall real nice for her. And she just got a bath, and guess what?"

"My, you have been busy while I've been gone." She brightened at the girl's approach.

He winced. Eloise had said "I" instead of "we."

"Rocco and Dr. Nate gave her a bath and she's a palomino! She's gold with a white mane, just like I wanted." Julianna's hand crept into Eloise's and clung tight. "Do you think she's the horse I prayed for? I love her so much."

"So I see." She gazed down at the child with gentleness.

What he saw on her face blew him away. He leaned against Licorice for support. She would make such a good mom. He had never had a thought like that about a woman. Not even Meryl, whom he'd planned to marry. It was strange how he would see Eloise as a mother, kind and patient and always smiling. He gulped, afraid to guess where this line of thought might take him.

"Sean? Are you all right, boy?" Uncle Frank strolled into sight, dapper in a new T-shirt and jeans as if he were ready for a date with Cady. "You're lookin' a mite pale."

"I'm fine. It's nothing." He glanced around, surprised they weren't alone. Aside from Julianna and Frank, there were a handful of other people in the aisle tending to the stabled horses. He spotted a couple of wall rings and drew a rein through one of them. "What's going on here?"

"It's Friday evening. I came by to pick up Cady for dinner and look at what I found." Frank was sharp-eyed. He didn't miss much. Along with the knowing grin was a look of understanding. "I thought I could lend a hand."

"Yeah. Me, too." Lending a hand, that sounded like as good a reason as any to be here. As long as he didn't have to admit to the truth. Eloise caught his attention as she followed Julianna through an open stall gate and closed it behind her. The palomino nickered gently and lowered her nose for the girl to pat. The mare closed her eyes, looking mighty glad to have attention.

Sean swallowed hard. Maybe his feelings had been

stirred up by coming across this kind of neglect; they had overwhelmed him. Perhaps that's all his new, tender feelings were toward Eloise. That meant their near-kiss was nothing more serious and neither was his glimpse of Eloise as a future mom. Wouldn't that be a relief?

"How did the horses ride?" A woman's voice drew him out of his thoughts.

The horses? He shook his head, realizing Cady was asking about the trip to and from town. He looped another rein through a ring and loosely tied it. "Good. I think Licorice is going to do just fine for you. Hershey might have a hard time adjusting to different riders. Maybe at first, maybe not. I can work with him if you'd like."

"Yes. Absolutely." Cady had a serene gentleness about her that made her likeable and a good match for Uncle Frank. "I would pay you."

"Not necessary." As if he would accept her money. If she could take in animals in need without complaint of the vet bills it might cost her, he could offer his time to help.

"Then perhaps you would accept goodies from the kitchen now and then." She strolled up in her designer boots to offer Hershey a hunk of carrot. "After all, you have to keep your strength up."

"I wouldn't argue that." Especially since everything that came out of the restaurant's kitchen was fantastic. He untied the sack of molasses treats from the back of the saddle and caught sight of Eloise in the stall with Julianna.

The rush of tenderness he'd felt at the street fair when he'd been a fraction away from capturing her lips with his hit him full force. He felt as if caramel were melting in the middle of his chest. It was friendship, that was all. It couldn't possibly be anything more. From here on out, he wouldn't let it be.

He hefted the feed bag on one shoulder and grabbed the pack of supplies in his free hand. Every step he took past Eloise, he wanted to look at her. He wanted to grin at her over the top of the stall gate and know what she was thinking by the set of her expressive eyes. He wished he could see the uptilt of her mouth without remembering what it had been like to almost kiss her.

He let the bag slide down to the floor in the feed room. Tucked out of sight from the breezeway, he didn't need to look up to know who was coming down the aisle in his direction. He recognized Eloise's gait and the faint tap of her cane on the concrete. He straightened up, and the melted caramel feeling in his chest increased as she approached.

"Oh, hi." She appeared startled to see him. "I'm leaving for the day."

"I guess it's quitting time already." He stood as still as stone. Not a muscle quivered. "Are you going back to the festival?"

"Not tonight." She took a step, hating that the palm of her hand had gone damp against her cane.

"Meeting someone?" He stepped into the aisle to call after her.

"You could say that." She didn't turn around. If she did, she would have to face him. "I'm having dinner again."

"Not another blind date?"

"Yes." She feared he saw her the way she saw herself—as someone with her best years behind her. Sean clearly was carried away when he'd tried to kiss her, but that didn't change the situation. Blushing, she took another step, painfully aware of the drag of her leg. Her limp would always be a part of her. She could not wish it away.

"Have a good evening, Sean," she called over her shoulder and kept going.

"I never thought that boy would leave," Frank quipped as he poured sparkling water into two crystal glasses.

"I think he's sweet on Eloise." Cady leaned forward on the blanket set in the soft green grasses in the shade of the stable to take one of the glasses.

"And then some." Frank grinned. He was sweet on Cady.

She was elegance in motion. Every little movement she made was graceful as if timed to music as she lifted the glass to her lips and sipped. The wind blew her soft brown hair against the side of her face and she brushed it away with her free hand before he could put down the bottle and do it for her.

"That's why I suggested they ride the horses to town to test them out." Cady traded her glass for her fork and daintily pierced a bow-tie pasta with the tines. "I thought the time together would do them good."

"Agreed. I think they need a push." He set down the bottle, making sure it didn't tip over in the uneven grass. He'd also liked Cady's suggestion they stay close to the horses instead of heading into town so the employee in charge of the barn could take a dinner break. He liked everything about her, especially her sensitivity to others. "Sean's been hurt, so he's holding back."

"Eloise, too."

"I know how that is." He took hold of his fork and loaded up. The meaty tomato sauce on the pasta was tasty and he ate so he didn't have to elaborate.

"Everyone knows what that's like." Cady's fork hovered in midair. "How long do you think it will be before he asks her out?"

"Probably not as long as it took me to ask you," he joked. He was always lighthearted with his Cady. He thought of her as his these days, not that he'd told her so yet. They had been having dinner and going riding for the past three months and each outing had gone well. Every time he was with her, he cared about her more. After being a widower for seventeen years, it was comforting to have someone to spend time with. Reassuring to know someone cared for him in return.

"You did take a long time." She laughed, nibbling on the pasta. She may have been a respected personal-injury attorney when she'd lived in New York, but he knew the reason she had been so successful was the quiet strength and steady kindness that shone from within her. It was easy to spot on an evening like this with the birds chirping and butterflies dancing from wildflower to wildflower. Her guards were down. Small-town life agreed with her.

"I didn't think you liked me at first," she confessed.

"Sure I did. What's not to like? I was fairly sure a gorgeous woman like you wouldn't look twice at an old rancher like me."

"Old?" That amused her. "Watch it, mister. If you are old at fifty-three, then I am old at fifty-one. I would rather not think of myself as old."

"I don't see you that way. True beauty is ageless and you are truly beautiful." He meant the words, but he also liked the way their impact moved across her face. Her honest eyes brightened and the radiance of her spirit somehow made her heart-shaped face more comely.

"You know how to charm a lady, Frank Granger."
She rose onto her knees with poise and brushed her lips
against his clean-shaven cheek.

"That's not the kind of kiss I was hoping for."

"It's not?"

"Maybe I should show you what I had in mind."

"Maybe." His kiss was perfection sugar-coated with
reverence. The brush of his lips to hers made her feel
cherished. His hand cupped her jaw, cradling her as the
sweet kiss lengthened. Her heart skipped three beats
from the sheer exquisiteness of his gentlemanly kiss.

No man ever had made her feel cherished the way
Frank did. Romantic love had eluded her all her adult
life, but no longer. It had found her in this little Wyoming town. Moving here to follow her dream of owning
a country inn had been the best decision of her life.

"Aunt Cady! Aunt Cady!" Julianna's voice echoed
through the stable's wide breezeway and across the
meadow full of wildflowers. The little girl burst into
sight, as dear as could be, skipping ahead of her sister
and father, Adam.

Love filled her as it always did for her goddaughters.
"Julianna. Why are you so excited?"

"Cuz Daddy said we can stay for another whole
week." She bounced to a stop at the edge of the blanket
and dropped to her knees. "Both Jenny and me. We can
stay if you say yes. Please, please, please?"

As if she had what it took to say no to those big
Bambi eyes and little girl fingers steepled as if in prayer.
She melted like an ice cube in Tucson.

"It's just us." Jenny, a serious twelve-year-old, tucked
a lock of dark hair behind her ear. "Daddy has to go
back to work."

"It's all he does," Julianna added sincerely as she

plopped down on the blanket and sidled close. "He's a workacolic."

"A workaholic," Jenny corrected coolly. "When we're home, he never spends time with us anyway, so we may as well stay here with you."

Cady recognized the hope buried in Jenny's aloofness, and it was just as strong as Julianna's glittery excitement. She wrapped her arms around the littlest girl, who was within reach, holding her close. These girls and their father were family.

Adam planted his hands on his hips and raised one eyebrow, and she recognized his grave look. She had seen it many times before. He had a hard time juggling single fatherhood, his demanding job as a cardiologist and the emotional aftermath of his divorce. He hadn't always been terribly somber. She gave Julianna another quick snuggle. "I would love to have you girls stay with me."

"Yay!" Julianna bounced happily. "I get to stay with Dusty. She needs me."

"I get riding lessons," Jenny announced primly, clearly trying hard to contain all her secret happiness.

"I'm getting the short end of the stick." Adam winked as he strode closer, no longer quite as somber. "Girls, let's leave Frank and Cady to their dinner. Sorry, we didn't mean to interrupt."

"No problem," Frank spoke up, easygoing as always. That was one thing she adored about him. He was a powerful and rugged man, and strong of character, too. Not much rattled him. He always went with the flow of things with good humor and steady confidence. "You're welcome to stay."

"Okay." Julianna bounced onto her knees to inspect the food and helped herself to one of the colorfully decorated cookies the inn's chef had packed in the picnic basket.

"I want one." Jenny dropped down to choose a cookie for herself.

"The more the merrier," Frank said, his deep baritone rumbling like a song. He winked, clearly not minding the intrusion. It was easy to see the father he'd been when his children were small, and the combination of might and gentleness made him more of a man in her eyes.

"This isn't the date you were hoping for." She lowered her voice, speaking over Julianna as the girl plunked down into Cady's lap. Adam came to peer into the basket too, interested in a selection of sliced fruit. She lightly wrapped her arms around the girl, holding her close. "First the horses and now this."

"Don't you worry about that. Any time I'm with you is a gift." So sincere. The power of his spirit made her world stop turning. He held out one big hand in silent invitation. "I'm glad to be here with you."

She laid her much smaller hand in his. Perfection. Their fingers linked, her soul stilled and she felt with her heart what he was too bashful to say with words.

Chapter Nine

Eloise. Against his will she dominated his thoughts on the drive home. As Sean cleaned and unhitched the horse trailer, images of the day with her overwhelmed him. Memories of her racing away from him on Licorice's back, the ring of her unguarded laughter, her look of shock when he'd tried to kiss her. He cringed and gave the garden hose a tug. He could still feel the imprint of her hand on his chest, blocking him from moving in to cover her lips with his.

He'd messed things up royally. He gave the nozzle a final blast, chasing the last of the soap bubbles from the tire rims. The trailer was clean inside and out and his work was done, but he didn't want to head down to the house. He knew it would probably be empty. He hadn't stopped by to see for sure on his way up the hill, but over breakfast this morning he'd overheard his cousins making plans to hit the street fair. Mrs. G. would have gone home. He didn't want to be alone battling thoughts of Eloise.

He coiled up the hose, working fast, trying to forget their awkward conversation in the inn's stable. When she'd walked away from him, it had felt final. He sighed, frustrated with himself. He hadn't even seen that attempted kiss coming.

A plaintive moo caught his attention. He glanced up. A white-faced Hereford leaned over the fence begging for attention. A half dozen other cows ambled over too, probably hoping for treats. He dug some out of the bag in the back of his truck and crossed the lane to greet them.

"Howdy, Buttercup." He rubbed her poll. She lowered her head to go after the treats. Being with animals made everything better. He chuckled as he held the goodies out of her reach. "You only get one, cutie. You have to share."

Buttercup's friends mooed in agreement and pushed against the fence too, eager for pats and treats of their own. Jasmine's long pink tongue stretched out. Lily, not to be outdone, caught hold of his T-shirt with her teeth and tugged.

"Girls, girls." He began handing out the treats since he was outnumbered. "There's enough to go around."

"You're popular with the ladies." Addy tromped into sight in the field, flanked by yearling cows who danced and hopped and skipped around her. "I can't believe you're not in town. Scotty can keep an eye on our expectant mare tonight so you don't have to stay. You should be having fun."

"I've already had all the fun I can handle." He held out the last of the treats to the cows, who devoured them cheerfully. He rubbed Buttercup's nose and Jasmine's poll. "Besides, the company is better here. Isn't that right, ladies?"

Buttercup mooed at him, as if in perfect agreement.

Addison laughed at the yearlings tumbling and playing around her and swiped a lock of straight strawberry-blond hair out of her blue eyes. "I've done nothing but work all day. Not that I mind but I'm dying to shop. I've got money to burn, or I will once I get a hold of Dad."

Addison reminded him again of his younger sister and he fought off a pang of homesickness. He missed his family. He was close to them. Maybe it was time for a call home. He put that on his mental to-do list. "The yearlings look good. They've been keeping you busy."

"Always. I've got the babies in the barn fed, so I'm heading down to the house." She patted a few eager heads. "Daisy, you be good while I'm gone. You too, Violet. Rose, don't even think about trying to get out of this fence. Are you sure you don't want to come?"

"I'll think about it." The evening was perfect, but the thought of spending it in an empty, echoing house made his stomach tighten. If he wanted to be a lone wolf, he would have to get used to it.

"C'mon. You really need to come." Addy climbed through the fence and bobbed to a stop beside him. "It won't be just us girls. We're all meeting up in front of the cotton-candy booth. Justin, Tucker and Ford will be there. You can hang with the guys."

"Good, because I don't think I could take hanging out with the likes of you." He gave her ponytail end a tug, just like he did when they were kids and was rewarded with her big, infectious grin.

"Fab! I'd better hurry. I promised I wouldn't be late." She took off at a dash down the lane. "Give me ten minutes, and I'll meet you at the truck."

"It'll be fifteen," he joked, as the cattle called out, saying goodbye in their cow-like way. His cell rang and drew their attention. Bovine ears pricked and eyes brightened in excitement as he fished it out of his pocket. Tongues reached, trying to grab the contraption from him and he chuckled. Cows were great.

He rubbed Lily's nose, stepped just out of reach of Buttercup's tongue. He expected to see his mom's number, but when he squinted at the display he couldn't believe his eyes. Meryl's name stared up at him. It was really her. She was calling. His palms went damp.

Three months ago, he used to pray for this. When his phone rang, it had been her name he had most wanted to see. Times had changed and he couldn't move his thumb to hit the button to answer the phone.

Something tugged at his hat brim. Teeth clamped on the neckline of his shirt. Yearling noses poked between the rails to sink their teeth into the legs of his jeans and tugged. The cows and their bright eyes were as affectionate as could be and a great comfort as he stared at the screen.

How could Meryl call after the way she'd left things? And why? It was like a sudden icy downpour had pummeled from the sky, drowning out the warmth and sunlight. He shivered in the eighty-degree temperature.

He hit Ignore and jammed the phone into his pocket safely out of sight but not out of mind.

"How did you like Craig?" Gran stepped onto the shaded old-fashioned porch with two glasses of icy lemonade in hand. The wooden screen door slapped shut behind her as she set the glasses on a pretty cloth-covered table. "Was he the one?"

"He was the last one." Eloise gave her car door a shove and trudged up the walk. Her weak leg seemed to drag more as she climbed the steps, but maybe it was her spirit that was lagging. She'd endured an hour and a half of Craig's flat monotone, his endless fascination with some video game he couldn't stop talking about and the fact that he looked just past her right shoulder whenever he spoke to her. Predictably he'd been quietly distasteful when he'd spotted her limp. Getting through that dinner had not been easy.

"No more, Gran. Take pity on me." She collapsed onto the closest cushion and leaned her cane against the side of the wicker chair. "Promise me you won't put me through another minute of this."

"I don't make promises I can't keep." Gran eased onto the neighboring chair. "Why is this so hard for you, sweet pea?"

"I would rather not talk about it. I'm here to weed." She had stopped quickly at home to change into an old T-shirt and shorts. She sipped the ice-cold lemonade and let the tangy sweetness sluice over her tongue. "I'm going to take this with me, though. Delicious."

"Don't you go anywhere, young lady. I already did the weeding." Gran's chin lifted with a touch of defiance. "I'm not too old yet to weed my tomatoes. Now, answer my question."

"I'd rather go back and have dinner all over again with Craig."

"Was it really that bad?"

"Gran, you are torturing me. The CIA could use this as a method for extracting information. It was agonizing." She may as well tell the truth. "Please stop fixing me up."

"What's so bad about meeting a nice young man?" Gran's face scrunched up, bewildered. "I know Craig had nice manners. I asked his grandmother to make sure."

"Yes, but you could have asked if he had a personality."

"Oh, my." Gran put her hand to her mouth and chuckled. "I had no idea he was lacking. I'll do better next time."

"Next time I'm going to bring you with me so you can see what I'm up against. There are no good men left." That was her argument and she was sticking to it.

"He is out there, mark my words." Her grandmother appeared certain, unfailing in her belief. "I've been praying."

"Fine, but can we change the subject?"

"The right man will love you the way you are, for all that you are." Gran took a dainty sip of lemonade.

I don't notice your limp. When I look, I see you. Sean's words rolled into her mind and so did the memory of the kiss they'd almost shared. She swallowed hard and set down her glass before she spilled it. She'd been terrified of his rejection. That was the reason she'd stopped him before his lips claimed hers.

What would his kiss have been like? She blocked her mind from envisioning that little scenario. Imagining the tender brush of his lips to hers would only make it harder to forget. She wanted to slap her forehead because she'd visualized exactly what she'd been trying to avoid—Sean's kiss.

"How did your date go with that nice Granger boy?" Gran asked as casually as if she'd asked about nothing more personal than the weather.

Eloise inhaled, sucking lemonade into the wrong pipe. She coughed and sputtered, gasping for air. Her face turned red. Her eyes watered. She could see the tip of her nose shining like a beet.

"It was not a date," she wheezed. A few chugs of lemonade got everything going the right way, but it didn't begin to soothe the turmoil roiling up within her. "Sean and I were taking two of the inn's new horses for a ride."

"I didn't see any horses."

"Trust me, it was work-related, not personal." Although it might have been. She gulped another swallow of lemonade, hoping Gran hadn't happened to witness their almost-kiss.

Maybe she had. Nothing went unnoticed in a small town. Gran looked merry over the rim of her glass. "You're a heartbreaker, Eloise. Just like me in my day. Oh, I had them lining up for me, too."

"I'm not sure I should be hearing this." She blushed harder.

"Your grandfather wasn't just the best of the bunch, he was simply the best. I knew it the moment I saw him. He was new to town, the owner of this ranch right here. I remember it as if it were yesterday. He moseyed into the diner and my heart stopped beating. Time stood still and I felt wonderful down to the soul. As if I had taken my first breath and my life was about to start anew."

"I know the story, Gran." Everyone in the family had heard it a hundred times, but it was sweet enough to savor again. "He looked at you, lifted his hat and told you he'd just met the lady he was going to marry."

"He did and I was charmed." Gran looked happy and sad in the same moment. Although Gramps was gone, her love for him had not dimmed. "I caught that Granger boy looking at you and I saw the same look in his eyes."

"Wishful thinking." Her heart felt ready to crack apart, which made no sense at all. Sean was *not* falling for her.

She grabbed her cane, gathering her dignity. Sean

had admitted he hadn't even meant to kiss her, and that was no surprise. She was painfully aware of the tap of her cane and her limping gait as she rose to fetch the pitcher from the kitchen. The breeze from the open windows scented the room with the fragrance of blooming flowers and warm summer air and made her rebellious mind boomerang right back to Sean, wondering what he was doing.

She hated to admit it, but she wasn't as unaffected by him as she wanted to be.

The muted light of evening hazed the town with a Norman Rockwell glow. Sean jumped into the back of the truck, since they'd picked up Cheyenne and Autumn in town. The last thing he wanted to do was to be stuck in the cab with three women bent on talking weddings. Not that he objected to matrimony, but a bachelor was required to avoid the topic. It was the manly thing to do.

"Are you sure you're okay back there?" Cheyenne peeked out the back window.

"I'm used to being hauled around like a bale of hay," he assured her. "It's how my family always treats me."

"Sure they do." Cheyenne laughed at him, shook her head as if to say there was no understanding the male species and told Addy to hit the gas.

The truck rolled forward away from the curb leaving the hubbub of the street fair behind. Some vendors had closed up for the day, others were doing a stellar business. In a few minutes' time, they hit the outskirts and the vehicle gained speed on the country road.

Since he had a moment to himself, he yanked his phone from his pocket. With the breeze whipping his face and hair, he studied the screen. One voice mail, it said. If he pushed the button, then he would hear her voice. He still smarted somewhat fiercely at the thought.

He drummed his thumb on his knee, debating. What did she want? If he deleted it without listening, he would never know. She might have apologized. Maybe listening to something like that would give him closure. Or, he thought with a leap of his pulse, she might want to get back together.

What do I do, Lord? He had moved on without Meryl and he was finally happy. Why mess that up?

Eloise. She was the one he wanted to talk with about this. She would understand. Was it wrong to want to see her? He frowned, belting out a frustrated sigh, angry with himself. After that debacle with the failed kiss, he didn't think he had the right to count on her friendship. He moved his thumb to the number pad of his phone, wishing he could call her.

He couldn't.

The truck swept around a long, lazy country corner heading directly into the sun. The shade from the cab fell over him, and his screen glowed brightly like a sign. He would face his problems on his own. He hit the voice-mail call button and waited, palms damp and respiration sketchy. Meryl's ingenuous alto lilted from the speaker.

"Sean. I know it's been a while and you probably don't want to talk to me. That's fine, I understand. I really do." Her voice hitched, as if she were in pain. "Please call me anyway. I need you to know how I feel. I made a mistake. A big mistake. Have you ever made one that you feel so bad about you are afraid nothing you can do will ever make it right? Well, that would be me. I'm praying there's a way to make things right, Sean. God is guiding me back to you."

A big mistake? He hit Delete. That tore him up. Things hadn't worked out with the dentist, huh? He was sorry for that, but he felt stirred up. The old wound became fresh.

This was why love was a bad idea. It should be avoided at all costs.

The back window slid open and Autumn smiled out at him. She shone with deep, contented happiness, the kind that polished her from the inside out. True love had done that. He was glad it had worked out for her. Concern creased her brow as she studied him. "Hey, are you all right?"

"I'm okay." He shrugged, hoping to dislodge the pain. It didn't work, but he wasn't ready to talk about it.

"I just heard the scoop about you and Eloise." She brushed her auburn curls behind her ear as the wind caught them. "I think it's great, by the way. We've all known Eloise forever."

"That's the way things go in a small town. People leap to the wrong conclusions awful fast." He loved this way of life, but he could use a little more privacy, at least where his heart was concerned. He'd taken two blows all in one day, first Eloise's rejection and now Meryl's apology, and it was about all he could take. "I'm just helping her with the inn's horses."

"It's so sad about those poor things." Autumn grew serious. "Is there something I can do?"

"You'll have to ask Cady. They're in relatively good condition, considering. No major illnesses, no injuries, and they are being well cared for now."

"Still, I feel like I should do something. Maybe I'll swing by the inn and see them."

"Sure." Inspiration hit. Maybe he should ask her to take over his offer to help Eloise instead. If Autumn stepped in, he could retreat into the background and keep his distance. It would be safer to bow out. It was a good idea, except for the matter of the quickly approaching wedding. As busy as Autumn was, he figured she would shuffle around her responsibilities.

He couldn't ask her. He couldn't say the words.

Chapter Ten

The Pioneer Days rodeo was in full swing. Eloise eased onto the hard bleacher seat, tucked her cane against her knee and resisted the urge to scan the rest of the arena for a certain somebody. Sean Granger was not on her mind—at least that was her goal.

"Oh, good, we haven't missed the barrel racing." Mom twisted open the small thermos she'd brought in a big wicker basket. "Do you want some, sweetie?"

"No thanks." While she listened to her mom pour a cup of iced tea to share with Dad, she did her best to watch the last of the event on the grounds below. Two riders on horseback swung lassoes after a wily black calf who was good at evading them.

"Oh, ho!" The announcer, Tim Wisener Junior, called out. "Looks like the Walters brothers have to try again." The speakers blared and echoed as the mid-afternoon heat blazed like an oven.

Just like old times. She found herself smiling. She'd forgotten all the many things she'd missed over the years about small-town life. A hometown rodeo was one of them. Half the county crowded onto the bleachers or milled around on the adjacent street. The wind brought the scents of dust, hay and popcorn from a nearby vendor's kiosk.

Everywhere she looked, she saw someone she recognized and exchanged smiles. Sierra Baker sat beside her fiancé, Tucker Granger, with her young son, Owen, tucked between them, pointing excitedly to the goings-on below. Sierra's parents, the Boltons, sat on the bench above. The group made a pretty picture of a family gathered for a fun day together and they weren't alone. Nearby Frank Granger sat next to Cady, surrounded by his family. Oops—she averted her gaze. Best not to look at that section of the bleachers where Sean was sure to be.

Down the row, she spotted the Parnell girls, all four of them blonde and as golden as could be, and her grandmother's friend, Mrs. Plum, sitting hand-in-hand with her husband of over fifty years. She noticed Jeremy Miller and his kids. The Bakers, Chip and Betty, looked happy and content surrounded by their immediate family. Their daughter, Terri Baker-Gold, sat with her husband radiating happiness, her hand resting lightly on the small bowl of her abdomen. Word had it their first baby was due in November.

So many happy families. Eloise blew out a breath but it didn't ease the painful tension bunched up in her chest. Since she knew who and what was responsible for it, she tried to ignore it. Not exactly easy, since every time she took a breath the tension refused to budge.

"Helene." A friendly woman's voice spoke from the row behind them. The scent of chocolate-chip cookies filled the air. Eloise glanced over her shoulder to see Martha Wisener holding an open plastic container full of treats. "Would you all care for some? I went on a baking binge this morning and made way too much."

"They look delicious," Eloise heard her mom say. "I'm going to get that recipe out of you one of these days."

"You and everyone else." Martha laughed. She tipped the container closer. "Eloise, you must have one. I've heard all about your quest."

"My quest? Do you mean finding the horses?" She thanked Martha and took a cookie. They looked buttery and chocolaty. How could anyone resist? She took a nibble and the soft chewy center and melty chips were bliss.

"Everyone's talking about it." Martha, who was also the mayor's wife and the town realtor, was up on all the latest news. She missed nothing. "I hunted down Cady a little bit ago to hear all about it. Abandoned horses. Such a terrible thing. I hear you were the one to find them."

"Actually, it was the humane society. They called me."

"Sad. I'm thankful they were found. Can you imagine? You just know God intervened at exactly the right moment. Any longer and who knows what would have happened to the poor things?" Martha tipped the cookie box in the other direction, offering it to Gran. "You have to be proud of your granddaughter, Edie."

"She's a keeper." Gran beamed sweetly. "How many horses are you going to find for Cady, dear?"

"I don't know. I'll stop when she tells me to or when the stable is full." The announcer hollered over the speaker, excited by a time earned by the next team-roping pair to finish—the Granger girls. Eloise turned back to her grandmother. "Knowing Cady, she will simply build another stable and fill that one also."

Down below, Addy lifted both fists in victory, while

Cheyenne coiled up her lasso and rode her horse toward the gate. Apparently the team had won. Eloise cupped her hands to her mouth. "Yay, Cheyenne! Yay, Addy!"

Her call was lost in the crowd, but she was happy for her friends and in that unguarded moment she forgot to keep her gaze averted from the section of bleachers directly ahead of her.

Sean. Her focus zoomed straight to him. He sat one row behind his uncle, his hat shading his rugged face. He was magnificent in a navy T-shirt shaping his impressive physique and jeans. So handsome, he made the knot in her chest multiply and she gasped for air. Time reeled backward and she remembered the moment on the street when he'd leaned in and she'd panicked.

What if she hadn't stopped him? The thought made her pulse bump to a stop. What if she had let him kiss her? Would he have pushed her away when he came to his senses? When the kiss was done and he stepped away, would he have regretted his impulsive act?

Probably. The sunlight glinted off her cane, propped against the bench beside her. What other outcome could there be?

His head shot up as if he'd sensed her interest and across the arena their gazes fused. The sounds and sights of the stadium faded until there was nothing but the intensity of his bold blue eyes rooting her into place. She could not move or blink, not even breathe. Could she rip her gaze away from his?

No. She felt an incredibly powerful pull on her heart, which felt like regret. She missed him. She remembered his stalwart kindness as he'd tended the starving horses and assisted the vet with competence and compassion. She recalled the strength in his arm when she'd needed to lean on him at the street fair when she'd forgotten her cane. Would his kiss have been gentle?

"Eloise?" Her gran's voice came as if from a far distance. "Is that Sean Granger? You should go say hi to the boy."

"N-no." The word stuck in her throat and sounded unnaturally loud and defensive. Oops, she hadn't meant to sound that way. She cleared her throat and tried again. "I mean, yes, it's him, but no, I don't need to say hi."

"Sure you do," Gran insisted. "After all the time you two have been spending together. You don't want to let a man like that get away."

"Get away?" She highly doubted she had a chance of ever holding Sean Granger. "He's just a friend."

"Famous last words," Martha interjected. "Although in this case, it might be wise. I hear he's nursing a broken heart."

"Eloise, you've been spending a lot of time with one of the Granger boys?" Mom sounded bewildered. "Why didn't I know that?"

"Because it's nothing." She wished she could focus on anything else but her gaze remained glued to his. Sean and his riveting blue stare, the strong lines of his face, the cut of his high cheekbones and the unyielding angle of his jaw—she couldn't see anything else.

They'd had fun together. She wished it could be more. But she had learned a painful yet important lesson from Gerald. Her disability was a liability to men. Hadn't all her blind-date fiascos proven it? No, she'd been right to stop Sean before he'd kissed her. They had to stay friends.

Tossing him an uncertain smile, she ripped her gaze from his. She felt winded from the superhuman effort that took, and her vision couldn't seem to focus on anything else. The blur of a horse and rider in the ring below would not become clear.

The barrel racing events had obviously started, but she hadn't heard Tim Wisener Junior announce it nor could she hear his comments as a horse spun around a barrel and knocked it over. Why couldn't she concentrate?

Because her attention was still on Sean. She could see him in the corner of her vision. He leaned forward, planted his elbows on his knees and rested his chin on his fists. He looked frustrated. He looked to be thinking. Was he regretting that she'd pushed him away? Or was he glad he hadn't kissed her?

You're not whole, Eloise. Gerald's words rolled up from her memory. *Nothing is ever going to change that. I can't keep pretending it doesn't matter. I've tried, I really have.*

She bowed her head, remembering how painful the lesson was. Her pink cane glinted in the sun, a reminder that her condition was never going to improve.

"Next up, we have Cheyenne Granger." Tim Junior's friendly tenor blasted across the open-air arena. "She's riding Dreamer, and she is our returning champion. Eight times she's won this event. Will she do it again? Here she comes, so let's find out."

Eloise swallowed and ate the remaining bite of the cookie before cupping her hands to cheer for her friend. When she was a girl, she used to race barrels and not well, so she knew it was harder than it looked. Cheyenne and her horse worked like a flawless team in a mad dash toward each barrel, each turn neat and tight before the all-out sprint for home.

"A new rodeo record!" Tim Junior proclaimed as the speaker crackled. "With a whole list of competitors to go, this is gonna get real interesting. Up next is Addison Granger. Let's see if she can steal the title from her big sister."

"Eloise?" A familiar baritone rumbled next to her ear. A familiar riding boot stepped into view.

Since her palms went damp and the knot sitting against her rib cage tightened, she didn't need to look to know who settled on the bleacher beside her.

"Are you enjoying the rodeo?" he asked in a low voice, perhaps aware of her family and Martha on the row behind them leaning just a bit to try to listen in.

"S-sure." The word caught in her throat. "Are you?"

"I always like a good rodeo. Look at Addy go." He nodded toward the ring where Addy's dappled gray American Quarter Horse executed a neat, hairpin turn around the second barrel. The crowd went wild as the mare dug in, stretched in an all-out sprint and pivoted around the final barrel. "She just might do it this year."

Sean's presence rattled her and she couldn't concentrate as Addy rode to the finish. Bless him for coming over and making the first move.

"I can't believe it!" Tim Junior's excitement echoed across the arena. "A tenth of a second short. Cheyenne holds on to first place, but barely. That was a great run, Addy! Next up we have Ashleigh Parnell—"

"I never apologized to you for the other day." Sean knuckled back his Stetson. "I should have and I didn't. I'm sorry."

"Don't worry about it. It's already forgotten."

"It is? Whew."

"Sure." She wanted those words to be true. She

showed how aloof and cool she could be, casual and unaffected. "It was no big deal."

"I think it was." He straightened his shoulders as if with an iron resolve. "It upset you and changed things between us."

"Everything is fine, Sean." She could practically see Martha Wisener ready to tumble off the edge of the bench straining to hear more. Gran wasn't even trying to mask the fact that she was eavesdropping.

Great. The last thing she wanted was for everyone to know what had happened. That Sean Granger *hadn't* kissed her. In the ring below, Ashleigh Parnell raced to the finish and Tim Junior belted out her time, the third best, a hair below Addison's. Eloise glanced down at her cane and wished with all her heart that she could be whole, the way she was before the accident. "Believe me, Sean, I understand completely."

"That's a relief. It won't happen again. One thing about me, I can be taught. I never make the same mistake twice."

"Then I guess we're still friends."

"Sure, you can't afford to stay mad at me."

"I wasn't mad at you."

"I have a horse trailer, remember? You need me."

"Cheyenne has a horse trailer, too. I could replace you."

"Don't do it. I'm a horse lover from way back. After finding those starved horses, I'm more committed than ever. This cause is too important to me." Even a lone wolf needed something to believe in and a purpose to his life. Even he needed a friend. As a small smile hooked the corners of her rosebud mouth and she returned her attention to the ring, he felt better. Happier.

Her Stetson shaded her lovely, wholesome face, and looking at her gave him a sweetly warm feeling.

He didn't want anything serious, so he figured it was wise not to analyze his feelings any further. This was friendship. That was his story and he was going to stick with it. Eloise clearly didn't feel anything else for him.

Good thing, he thought ignoring a sting of disappointment, the lone wolf he was determined to be.

Tim Junior belted out the name of the next contestant and the noise and commotion of the spectators reminded him they were far from alone. An electronic jingle interrupted whatever it was Sean had been about to say. He tugged his cell from his jeans pocket and answered the call. It was from the ranch. "Scotty?"

"Sunny's finally decided to have her foal. Of course it's when everyone but me is away."

"That's the way it always works." A foaling mare he could handle. "Did you call Nate?"

"Yep, got him in the stands a few minutes ago."

Sure enough, a Stetson-wearing man was making his way through the grounds. Nate, off to the Granger ranch. Sean set his shoulders. The timing was bad, but duty called.

"How are the girls doing at their events?" The long-time ranch hand was practically a member of the family.

"So far, Cheye and Addy have come in first in their team events, first and second in their individual ones." He tried to focus on what he was saying, but Eloise stayed on the forefront of his thoughts. Her brow furrowed, a question pinched the corners of her eyes, and she leaned toward him with concern. He tried to focus. "Does Uncle Frank know?"

"You were the one on call, so I dialed you first," Scotty explained.

"Good, let him enjoy his date with Cady. I'll be right there." He pocketed his phone, hating to have to leave Eloise. He wanted to fix what was wrong between them.

"You have to go?" she asked.

"Sunny has decided to have her foal." Bad timing, he thought, tugging out his keys. But then again, God's timing was always perfect and that gave him an idea. "Want to come?"

"With you?" Surprise twinkled like pretty spring-green specks in her eyes.

"Why not? Don't you want to see a little foal born? I'll let you pet the baby."

"I'm not tempted." Her resistance was melting. He could see it as she tugged her bottom lip between her teeth, debating.

He didn't want to leave without her.

"C'mon, Eloise." He held out his hand, palm up. "Cute little foal. How can you resist? Maybe we should take a poll."

"A poll?" Amusement stretched her soft mouth into a dazzling smile.

He glanced around for support. He didn't have to look far. Martha was balancing precariously on the bench one row up. Eloise's mom had a pleasant smile of surprise. Mrs. Tipple seemed about ready to burst with excitement. Looked like he had all the backing he needed. "What do you all think? Should Eloise come along with me or keep hanging out with you?"

An easy question, since he already knew the outcome. Eloise knew it too, judging by the way she shook her head at him, scattering the ends of her gleaming gold hair.

"Don't you bring my family into this," she warned, but it was too late.

"I'll choose for you," Mrs. Tipple called out. "Eloise, looks like you've got a live one."

"I'm not fishing, Gran." Eloise bit her bottom lip, as if holding back a laugh. Merriment made her brilliant and made his heart notice. "And if I was, then I would throw him back. You do that with the ones too scrawny to keep."

He liked that everyone laughed. He laughed, too. He knew good and well he wasn't scrawny.

"You've hooked a good one." Martha leaned in. "Eloise, you don't let him get away."

"I haven't hooked him." She grabbed her cane and pushed off the bench. "If I wanted to hook some man, I could do better."

"You definitely could," he agreed and held out his hand to help her down the crowded aisle. Funny how calm he felt the moment his fingers twined between hers, like everything was going to be all right.

"You two have fun," her grandmother called and gave two thumbs-up. "I think it's a date, Helene. It looks like one to me."

"I hope you didn't hear that." The breeze scattered Eloise's gossamer wisps of gold curls that had tumbled down from her pony tail. "You know about my grandmother's plan to marry me off, right?"

"How could I forget? She's responsible for your last two dates." He led the way down the row, excusing them as he went. A lot of inquisitive gazes took note as they made it down the steps. "I saw her two thumbs-up. I rate better than I thought."

"Don't take it personally. Remember George? She gave him two thumbs-up, too."

He chuckled, protecting her from the tussle of the stragglers heading into the grandstand. It was a perfect afternoon without a cloud in the sky. He felt as bright as the sun and with Eloise beside him, his world seemed promising. As much as he wanted to deny it, his feelings were changing against his will.

Chapter Eleven

What she liked most about Sean could be best seen in the little things he did, Eloise decided as she clutched the top rung of the gate in the Grangers' main horse barn. She couldn't tear herself away from the sight of him kneeling inside the birthing stall with the vet, the mare straining in the throes of her contractions. This was a deeper side of Sean than she'd seen before, mighty and yet calm, sure of himself in a humble but amazing way.

"You're doing good, Sunny." Sean stroked the horse's neck like the accomplished horseman he was, his tone soothing and musical. "What a good girl you are."

She'd seen foalings before but each one was special. She loved watching Sean be part of it. She was fascinated by the unfaltering comfort he gave the mare. His capable manner gave the horse confidence.

"I've got two hooves," Nate announced in a steady, assured voice. He gently uncurled a leg and held the two tiny hooves in his palms.

"You're doing great, Sunny," Sean encouraged. "Your baby is almost here."

Good decision to come along, she thought. She wouldn't trade this for anything.

The man belonged in this environment, with the sun slanting over him and the soft straw beneath his boots. She remembered the way he'd helped her into the truck back in town, his care as he found the seatbelt for her and closed her door. He lived with confidence and thoughtfulness. Everything he did, he did well, big tasks or small ones, important or insignificant. His good heart shone through.

Very, very hard not to admire that.

"Is she here?" A little girl's voice echoed down the breezeway, followed by an older sister's scolding *Shhh!*

"Hush, Julianna. You are supposed to be quiet or you'll scare Sunny." Footsteps tapped closer. "She's having a baby, you know."

"I know, Jenny. Frank said I get to name her."

"He said *we* get to name her."

Both of the Stone girls tromped into sight with identical dark brown hair and beautiful button faces. Julianna's pigtails bounced with her gait, while Jenny's dark locks were sleek and freshly tended to. She slipped her comb into her pocket. "Hi, Eloise," they said in unison.

"Come see." She inched aside to make room for the girls. With one final thrash, a tiny brown bundle tumbled into the straw at Nate's knees.

"Wow." Julianna curled her fingers around the gate rung. "Look at the baby."

"It's so cute." Jenny stared, unblinking.

The baby studied them all with a startled look. Fuzzy ears stood straight up as the newborn took in its new surroundings. Inside the stall the mother rested, catching her breath.

"We've got a little filly," Sean announced as he gave the mare one last neck pat and strolled up to the gate. "Do you girls have a name picked out?"

"Tomasina," Julianna announced.

"Angelina," Jenny argued.

"I guess you two have some negotiating to do." He climbed between the rungs, broad-backed and with every muscle rippling. At his six-foot-plus height, he towered over her, a giant of a man in her estimation.

Such a good man.

"Are you glad you stayed?" he asked, smiling because he already knew the answer. Somehow, he knew. Although several feet separated them, the distance shrunk.

"Very." Danger, her instincts shouted at her, but did she listen?

No. It was impossible to see anything else but Sean.

"What's going on here?" a man's baritone boomed cheerfully. Frank Granger, hand in hand with Cady, ambled into sight.

"We've got ourselves a new filly," Sean answered, staying close, his hand gently closing around the curve of her shoulder to keep her from sidling away.

Panic popped like little bubbles in her midsection. At least, she thought it was panic. Maybe it was better not to analyze her feelings too much.

"So I see." Frank Granger with Cady at his side stopped to peer in over the bars. "Good job, Sunny girl. That's a fine baby you've got."

The mare lifted her head, her dark eyes finding Frank. She nickered low in her throat in answer and rolled off her side onto her folded legs.

"The baby is so pretty," Julianna chimed in. "Can we pet her?"

"Not yet, Julianna," Jenny answered.

"Maybe in a bit," Frank said.

Eloise tried to focus on the animals inside the stall, but the pressure of Sean's hand on her shoulder riveted her attention to him. She could hear the faint regular rhythm of his breathing. She couldn't help noticing the dark blue specks in his irises and the five-o'clock shadow beginning to darken his iron jaw.

"Look! She's getting up!" Julianna clung to the gate, fascinated as the mare climbed to her feet and gave the top of her baby's head a lick.

The filly blinked, still busy taking in her new surroundings. Nothing could be more adorable than her perfect dishpan face, long lashes and big chocolate fudge eyes. Her mane was short and coarse, sticking up like broom bristles. A white star crested her forehead.

"I've never seen anything so precious," Cady cooed.

"We get a lot of that around here. Every single foal is precious." Frank looked content with the life he had built here, but it was a different kind of contentment that lit him up when he looked at Cady.

True love. It was easy to see, and no one deserved it more.

"Oh, we missed it!" Addy interrupted, tromping in, followed by her sisters.

"Only by a few minutes." Sean didn't remove his hand and he didn't step away, but held her in place—not that she was complaining—as Cheyenne and Autumn ambled into sight, trailed by the rest of the Granger family. Justin appeared, walking hand in hand with his wife, Rori. Tucker came last with six-year-old Owen riding on his shoulders and Sierra by his side.

"Good job, Sunny." Autumn ducked between the rails. The mare nickered in greeting and proudly licked her filly's face as if to show off the baby. "She's a beauty, just like you."

"Aren't you glad you came?" Sean whispered so only she could hear.

"Maybe," she hedged but inside she thought, *definitely*. Tingles skidded down her spine, which probably came from standing so still for so long. That combined with the excitement of the newly born foal, well, that was probably the explanation. Those tingles had nothing to do with Sean.

"I get to do this for a living." He looked pretty happy with that.

"You are blessed. Not everyone can say the same." A wisp of sleek gold slipped from beneath her hat to fall in her eyes. He brushed it away, letting his fingertips linger on the silken skin of her forehead.

Another little tingle, but surely it could not be from the sweetness of his touch.

"I consider myself a pretty fortunate man," he went on. "As long as Uncle Frank decides to keep me on. This is a temporary position."

"Yes, we all know." Frank chuckled easily and winked. "Temporarily is about all I can put up with you, boy."

"So everyone tells me." He shook his head, his dimples dazzling.

Those handsome dimples would make any female in the state of Wyoming notice, so it wasn't anything to worry about. No reason to read anything into her reaction. That was probably the hazard of having a drop-dead gorgeous guy for a friend.

"Why do you think I'm here? My parents wanted to get me out of the house." That made everyone chuckle in agreement, although beneath the banter there was a loving acceptance of Sean that was hard to miss.

"Answer a question that is puzzling me," Cheyenne asked, turning to her. Friends that they were, it was easy to recognize the sparkle of amusement in Cheyenne's blue eyes. "Why are you putting up with our cousin? Surely there is some better guy to hang out with."

"You know it." Eloise felt more lighthearted than she had in years as the wind gusted down the breeze-way and the filly splayed out her thin, impossibly long legs. "I keep him around mostly because of his horse trailer."

"That explains it." Frank Granger roared. "We have all been wondering what a fine gal like you is doing with the likes of that boy."

"I'm the disappointment of the family," Sean explained with a shoulder shrug, as if it didn't trouble him one bit. "It's always a topic at all the family get-togethers."

"Better you than me," Addy quipped, hanging off the rail beside the little girls.

"I have a horse trailer," Cheyenne chimed in. "Now you don't have to hang with Sean."

"True, but I come with mine lickety-split whenever she calls." Sean winked. "I'm no dummy."

Everyone's laughter rang merrily in the barn, and he didn't mind that they were all laughing with him. He caught the look in his uncle's gaze, the one that said, "Told you so."

Uncle Frank was wrong. Everyone was. Even if his

feelings were starting to change, it didn't matter. He had supreme self-control. He was in charge of his feelings. No problem.

"Eloise, why don't you stay for supper?" Uncle Frank asked in that sly, knowing tone. "We've got plenty, and you haven't lived until you've tasted Mrs. G.'s potato salad."

"I don't see how I can say no to that," she said. "Only someone particularly daft turns down the chance for some really great potato salad."

"My sentiments, exactly," Sean added, fighting a brightness taking root in his heart he did not wish to claim.

At least the tingles in her spine had stopped and Eloise took comfort in that. She swiped the dishcloth across the kitchen table, brushing up crumbs from a tasty and fun supper. That was the Granger way, she'd learned long ago. Good food, better conversation and the family's lively interaction had been more entertaining than the rodeo. Even cleanup was fun.

"Mrs. G. works too hard," Cheyenne said from the sink where she was dealing with the hand washables. "We should do something for her."

"Dad pays her. A lot," Addy spoke up, standing next to her sister and drying dishes. "I caught a glimpse of the check he writes her every week. Wow."

"She earns it." Rori set the last of the leftovers into the refrigerator with orderly care. "Don't think it's easy taking care of all of you. I've done it, so I'm speaking from experience."

"We *are* a tough bunch." Autumn sidled up to Rori at the refrigerator and snagged a bag of carrots from the produce drawer. "I think we should do something for Mrs. G., too. Maybe a day at Cady's spa."

"Ooh, that's a great idea." Addy gleamed with enthusiasm. "We should all go."

"You just want to be pampered," Cheyenne argued with a laugh. "We're talking about Mrs. G. here, not you."

"I know, but I was just saying." Addy grinned sweetly and popped a plastic colander, newly dried, onto the counter. Sierra swept it up and put it away.

"I agree with you," Sierra put in her two cents' worth. "I could use a little pampering, too. Why limit it to Mrs. G.?"

Amused, Eloise scoured away gravy drippings and cherry pie filling that had landed on the vinyl cloth during the meal. The TV in the next room blasted a Mariners game, the noise only to be outdone by the outcry of the men seated around the room, bummed at an umpire's call.

No one else in the kitchen reacted to whatever was going on in the living room, but if she leaned slightly to her right she could see a sliver into the living room where Sean sat, leaning forward on the sectional, elbows on his knees, groaning along with his cousins and uncle. His dark hair stood on end, tousled as if he'd run his fingers through it in frustration.

"Yes. Doesn't Mrs. G. live all alone?" Cady said as she swiped a cloth over the countertops. "She might like a girls' day out instead of going to the spa all by herself. It's always fun hanging out with you Granger girls."

"We are keepers," Addy piped up cheerfully.

"*We* are, but not you, little sister," Cheyenne teased.

"Hey! You splashed me."

"Then you owe me a splash."

"Don't think I won't forget," Addy warned, glittering with humor. "Sometime in the near future when you least expect it. Splash!"

"Ooh, I'm scared." Cheyenne rolled her eyes and drained the sink. "Eloise, are you okay?"

Vaguely she heard her name as if from a great distance but she was too busy watching Sean rock back against the cushions looking unhappy. His team must not be doing well. He was terribly handsome, even when bummed. The strong blade of his nose and the chiseled cut of his jaw could have been carved out of marble. No man had ever captivated her the way he did.

"Eloise?"

A touch brushed against her shoulder and she startled, gazing up into Cheyenne's concerned blue eyes. How long had she been staring at Sean? Heat crept across her face. "Sorry. I guess I was staring off into space."

And at a really amazing guy, but she kept that part to herself.

"I do that all the time," Addy commented across the kitchen as she hung up the dish towel on the oven handle.

"Sure, you do." Cheyenne's gentle teasing held a note of caring. "But Eloise has more common sense than you."

"Hey!" Addy countered good-naturedly.

"Is your injury bothering you?" Cheyenne asked with a good friend's concern and a doctor's skilled eye. "You have been on your leg all day."

"I'm fine." Her weak leg was a little prickly from so much activity but that wasn't out of the ordinary. Her neurologist had said she would always face limitations, and she was deeply grateful to God that those limitations weren't what they once were. At least for now. "I'm just overwhelmed by you all. It's been a while since I've hung out with the Grangers."

"We are a rowdy bunch," Cheyenne agreed. "Not me, but others are."

"I am, definitely," Autumn chimed in with a bag of carrots in hand. "Anyone want to come with me to the barns?"

"Me!" Addy called out. "I want to see how the new baby is doing."

"Me, too," Cady said above the sudden jingle of a cell phone in the adjacent mudroom. "Oh, I think that's mine."

"Look at Dad," Cheyenne whispered as Cady slipped from the room. "He doesn't want us to know, but he's keeping an eye on Cady. He's always aware of her."

"They seem really serious." Eloise managed to find the words, but she couldn't take her attention away from Sean. Distantly, she realized the dishcloth was missing from her hand.

"Dad is completely head over heels when it comes to Cady." Cheyenne balled up the cloth and tossed it. It sailed across the island to land in the sink.

"Two points." Addy headed to the living room, gripped the sides of the archway and leaned in, pitching her voice to be heard above the roar of the game. "I know it's exciting in here and everything, but we're heading out. Anyone want to come?"

"It's batter up," one of the brothers said.

"Yeah, bases loaded." Little Owen's sweet voice made everyone smile. "Tucker and me gotta see what's gonna happen next. Then can we go to the barn?"

"Then we can go, buddy." The love for his soon-to-be stepson was impossible to miss.

More conversations rose up, but Eloise heard nothing other than silence as Sean rose from his seat. The distance between them zoomed like a camera in a movie, focusing in until there was no one in the house, no one in the room but him and his slow, incredible smile. Dimples framed the corners of his mouth like a dream, stealing her breath. She leaned on her cane, a little dizzy, a little overwhelmed. Her pulse tripped over itself as she grabbed the edge of the table for balance. Strange how he affected her equilibrium, and it worsened as he paced closer. His bright blue gaze latched onto hers with uncomfortable intensity.

Why was the tingling back? Shivers snapped like bubbles in her spinal column. She gulped, realizing she was alone to face Sean's approach. Cheyenne had moved away and headed toward the back door with her sisters.

"You look like you're having a good time." He ambled up. "Although it can be overwhelming. This branch of the Granger family is just plain crazy."

"In the best possible way." She didn't remember deciding to join him. She fell in stride beside him. The sunshine slanting through the wide picture windows brightened inexplicably. "This reminds me of all the times I stayed over with Cheyenne for supper and sleepovers when we were kids."

"Good times?"

"The best. I come from a big family too, so I'm used to all the action."

"Life would be dull without it. That's the problem with being a lone wolf." He held the screen door for her.

"*You* are a lone wolf?"

"Don't act so surprised. I thought my solitary wolf thing showed."

"Not even close."

"Really? I was sure I radiated aloofness." Those dimples ought to be illegal in every corner of Wyoming. "I'll have to try harder."

"Much harder." Her cane tapped on the porch boards.

At the rail, Cady smiled as they passed, phone to her ear.

"Yes, Adam. The girls are doing fine. No, Jenny was a gem today. As happy as could be. You're still coming to pick the girls up on Friday?"

"Daddy! Daddy!" Julianna dashed up the steps with a clatter, hand held out for the phone. Jenny jogged behind her at a slower pace, but judging by her look she was eager to talk to her father, too.

Such nice little girls. Eloise couldn't help feeling a little wishful. She'd always planned on having kids one day, always wanted to be a mom. She leaned on her pink walking stick on the way down the steps. No man was going to marry her now, so motherhood wasn't going to happen. It was another loss she had to learn to live with.

"I don't know how anyone is going to tear Julianna away from the horse she rescued." Sean matched his pace to hers as they crossed the lawn. "The Stone family should just move out here."

"I agree. She and Dusty are bonded. It's been adorable to see how they need each other." She glanced over her shoulder to watch the girls trade the phone back and forth, the din of their merry chatter as sweet as lark song on the breeze.

"Their father might not be as interested in moving here."

"Why not? He's a surgeon. We could use one of those in these parts. There are a few specialists over in Sunshine, but mostly we have to go to Jackson, Boise or Salt Lake City. When Owen had his heart surgery, Sierra took him to Denver."

"I remember. I had just landed the job with the inn at the time." She wondered how difficult it had to be for Adam Stone to be separated from his children. His daughters clearly loved him, chattering merrily away, eager for the chance to tell their dad everything they had been up to.

A cow's moo cut through her thoughts.

"We're coming, Buttercup. No one has forgotten you." Sean chuckled. "Buttercup is my sweetie. Isn't that right, girl?"

The cow lowed, pleased with her status as Sean's beloved. She wore a necklace of buttercups. A single daisy was stuck jauntily on the fluffy tuft of hair between her ears. Clearly Julianna and Jenny had been spending time with her before their father's call. Buttercup's big puppy-dog eyes beamed as she placed her nose in Sean's outstretched hands and sighed with emotion at seeing him again.

"You have a way with the ladies," Eloise quipped. "Too bad it's only with the bovine variety."

"It's my lot in life." He winked, unaware of the image he made with the sun's low rays painting him in a golden glow. "That's why I'm a lone wolf. It didn't always used to be by choice."

Buttercup batted her long curly eyelashes at him and

lipped at the collar of his T-shirt. She drew the fabric into her mouth, holding on tight to him, adoringly.

Yeah, Eloise thought, she knew just how Buttercup felt.

Chapter Twelve

The sound of voices filled the breezeway as Sean knelt to check Wildflower's cinch. The mare watched him curiously, her ears twitching as she listened to the rise and fall of familiar voices a few feet away. He resisted the urge to pick out one soft alto among all the others just like he was doing his level best not to let his gaze drift over the horse's gold rump to where the women congregated in front of Sunny's stall, cooing over the newborn foal.

Lone wolves did not moon after pretty gals. They stayed remote, defenses up, in control of their common sense.

Satisfied the cinch was tight enough, he patted the mare's neck.

"Looks like we're ready to go," he told the mare. "You don't mind taking Eloise home, do you?"

Wildflower, the good girl that she was, whickered low in her throat, an affable agreement. He walked behind her, placing a hand on her flank and did the same to his gelding, Bandit, who arched his neck and stomped his foot, eager to go. He'd spent the day in his corral, and he was a horse that liked to stay busy and on the move. Sean knew just how he felt.

"Don't worry, we'll head out in a minute, buddy, I—" He looked up, spotted Eloise, and forgot whatever else he'd been meaning to say.

She blew him away. Slim and willowy, she leaned against the gate, transfixed by the foal, wonder on her face. She was golden goodness as she glided her fingertips across Star's forehead—Julianna and Jenny had agreed on the name for the new filly.

"Hi, little one." It was her musical words that stopped him in his tracks, her delight that stole the air from his lungs. Happy, she glowed as bright as the sun's rays slanting through the open door, a rare and arresting beauty. The newborn foal's eyes drifted shut at her tender touch.

"She likes you, Eloise," Cheyenne said, and Addy chimed in something too but he didn't register what.

It was nearly impossible to hear a thing over the rush of his pulse thudding in his ears like a death knell.

"I don't know how you Grangers get any work done." Eloise stopped stroking and the foal's eyes opened.

"It's tough," Cheyenne agreed. "There's nothing but foals in the fields with their dams and calves in the pastures with their mamas. Most days all you want to do is play with the little ones."

"She is amazing, wobbling on those long, awkward legs. Adorable."

"I don't know how many foals have been born on his ranch, and I am in awe every time," Cheyenne agreed. "They are so innocent and sweet and knock-kneed. Just too cute."

Cute, sure. He was in awe, totally. But it wasn't the foal that captivated him. Not even close. Eloise's gentle laughter radiated joy as the filly clamped onto the hem of her pink T-shirt with her velvety muzzle. With care, Eloise gently freed her shirt from the little darling's clutches.

Something nudged his hand, dragging him out of his reverie. It was Sunny, who gave him a look that plainly said she was waiting.

"Sorry, girl." He tugged a chunk of carrot out of his pocket. She grasped it with her big horsy teeth and her whiskers tickled his palm. As she crunched contentedly, his attention drifted back to Eloise. "Are you ready to head home?"

"I'm not sure I can tear myself away." Elation rolled through her words.

"I can't compete. I'm definitely second fiddle to a filly like Star." He approached the throng of women, knowing full well what his cousins thought about his friendship with Eloise, but he didn't let other people's suspicions bother him. "We can stay here as long as you want, but I've got the horses saddled and ready."

"I don't want to make them stand too long. It's a beautiful evening." Eloise swept a lock of silken hair behind her ear and pushed away from the bars. "I wouldn't want to be tied up in the stable, not on an evening like this. Goodbye, little baby."

The foal's ears swiveled, taking in the sounds. Her chocolate fudge eyes were wide and curious as she watched the human walk away from her. Her mother, at her side, gave a low whicker of reassurance. His cousins called out their goodbyes and Eloise returned them. Could he listen? No, not with Eloise at his side.

"I saddled Cheyenne's saddle horse, Wildflower, for you." He slowed his gait to match her uneven one.

"Hey, girl." She held out her free hand for the mare to scent. "We know each other from way back, don't we?"

In answer, Wildflower lowered her head for a scratch, which Eloise obliged. His spirit brightened simply from watching her.

"I thought that might be the case." He knelt and laced his fingers together. "Need a boost?"

"No, but since you are already down there…" Trouble twinkled along with dark green flecks in her irises as she turned her attention to him. "You may as well make yourself useful."

"Useful." The full focus of her gaze walloped him, leaving him breathless. It was all he could do to stay steady as she planted her foot in the palms of his hands. "Glad to know I'm good for something around here."

"Oh, I'm sure you must have some value in addition to being useful."

"If I do, that's news to me." He lifted effortlessly, boosting her into the saddle. "If I have so much value, you might have to hang out with me more often."

"I'm not sure I would go that far." Leather creaked as she settled into place, towering like a princess on a throne.

"It seems to me if I have such merit you wouldn't hesitate." He snatched the cane she'd left behind and tucked it behind the saddle, then tightened the ties until it was secure.

"Oh, there's the male ego. I knew it was there. Every man has it."

"Please, don't go confusing me with other guys. I'm not that bad, am I?" He untied Wildflower's right rein from the wall hook and drew it up for Eloise to take.

"I said you had some merits. That doesn't erase your

many, many flaws." Dimples hooked the edges of her pretty mouth.

No one could make him laugh the way Eloise could. He untied Bandit and swung into the saddle. "Fine, I have a few flaws. More than a few flaws. See, I'm better than other men since I can admit it."

"Yes, clearly superior."

His big black gelding tossed his head, ready to roll. Sean pressed his heels and the horse responded, eager to get out in the summer evening.

Birds chirped and flitted from fence post to tree. Horses grazed. In the fields far up the hillside cattle lounged, looking like a mass of black dots against the stunning grassland. The clomp of hooves as he and Eloise rode together down the hill was about the most companionable thing he'd ever known.

Now this is friendship, he thought, watching the gentle breeze flutter through the ends of Eloise's hair. He and she were two like souls out for a ride, enjoying the summer evening. He wasn't noticing in the slightest that she was the most beautiful woman in the world. He'd hardly even glanced at her soft rosebud mouth upturned in a smile. As for his crazy attempt to kiss her?

Forgotten. Wiped from his memory permanently.

"Let's cut through the fields," he suggested. It was shorter than following the roads to her house and more scenic.

"Just what I was thinking." She tugged the brim of her Stetson lower against the sun. "It's a perfect evening for riding."

"That it is." Perfect. That was the exact word he'd been searching for. Nothing could be finer than being on the back of his horse with her riding at his side. He breathed in the fragrance of the windswept meadows and felt her shadow fall across him as he sidled Bandit up to the gate to unlatch it.

"I was just wondering why Buttercup wasn't dashing up to us." Eloise rode past him into the field, stirring his heart like ripples in a pond.

Remember, you don't feel a thing, he told himself and followed Eloise into the pasture. Feelings were what got a man into big trouble. Heartbreak trouble. He swung the gate closed behind him. The horse waited with a swish of his tail while Sean secured the latch and double-checked it.

"No wonder," Eloise said as if from a thousand miles away. It was hard to hear anything over the crazy drumming in his ears. She sat straight in her saddle, gently gorgeous and quietly dazzling. "The girls are busy adoring Buttercup appropriately."

"That cow is the most spoiled bovine in the state. Maybe in the entire country."

"Perhaps the whole continent?"

It took all his effort to focus on the gathering at the far end of the field, since his eyesight seemed fixated on Eloise against his will. He tried to focus on the two little girls flanking tall, slender Cady, but everything was blurry. The trio were petting Buttercup and adding a crown of daisies to the top of her head. "There ought to be a law."

"Yes, animal pampering ought to be regulated," she quipped, although a layer of seriousness remained beneath.

He knew what she was thinking. He winced because he didn't think he could ever get the sight of those half-starved horses out of his head. That had been an emotional day. Proof that emotions were best avoided, since they had led to his disastrous attempt to kiss her. From here on out, no emotions allowed. "Here's my law. All animals should be pampered."

"I would vote for it. That's always been my rule." She patted Wildflower's neck and the mare nickered as if she were in total agreement, too.

"That's why I love working with Uncle Frank." He steeled his chest so no emotions could sneak in and cause all sorts of trouble. "I love ranching, I love working outdoors, I love cows. I could have hired on at a lot of other big operations in the state. There are always openings."

"But you wanted to work with your uncle."

"Yes. Not just because he's my dad's brother, but because of what he stands for." He liked that Eloise understood that and understood him. He relaxed a little, rocking in the saddle slightly in time with Bandit's gait. "He's a top-notch rancher and he treats his animals right."

"You want to learn from him."

"I want to be like him." He kept his attention on the ground ahead where a worn trail wove its way through the tall grass and nodding wildflowers. Amazing that Eloise could instantly see what his parents had not been able to get. "He has a gift with animals, and he's good to them. He respects them. There's never a harsh word used, never a whip, never an electric cattle prod. Every steer, cow and calf has a name and they aren't solely a means to making a profit, but they are the point of the ranch. There is a reward in ranching the right way that no amount of money made can begin to compete with."

"Sounds noble to me."

"Glad you think so." Her opinion mattered to him. He let silence settle between them, broken only by the occasional creak of a saddle and the rhythmic plod of horse hooves. Bandit's mane rippled when he lifted his head to scent the wind. Wildflower danced closer to avoid a sudden flurry of a killdeer bursting out of the grasses and crying out, feigning an injured wing to lead them away from her nest.

"I think that's the secret to a happy life." She didn't rein Wildflower away but let the mare walk alongside Bandit, so close Sean could reach out and catch her hand with his.

Not that he wanted to hold her hand. But he could.

"What's the secret?" he asked.

"That happiness can't be found necessarily in the big successes of life or the material benefits, but in the things that can't be measured. In knowing you are doing things the right way. Living your life with honor. Living with your heart." She caught her hat with one hand as she tipped her head back, breathing in the scent of the winds and letting the gold-layered sun rays paint her with sepia tones. "It's also pretty nice riding horses on an amazing summer evening like this."

"It is pretty amazing. The evening, I mean. The horse ride." And her. She was awesome and so full of life that her emotions tugged him along with her, forcing him to feel. Not the easy things like the warmth of the sun on his face, but the hope that could be found when he peeled back the scars on his heart and looked beneath the surface.

"It's what I've been struggling with," she confessed. "I've had so many losses since the accident, not just having to give up skating."

"It sounds to me like you had to give up every-thing."

"Not everything, but it felt that way. One day my life

was going great. The next what I'd worked for so hard for years was gone. My career, my life in Seattle, my relationship with Gerald." Along with the chance to be married, to be a mom and raise kids of her own, but she couldn't admit that aloud. Not to Sean. Not to anyone.

The pink glint of sunshine hitting her stowed cane was the reminder of why. Seated in a saddle, her disability didn't show, but would always be with her and always a part of her. She set her chin, determined to stay positive. "Somehow I have to live with those losses and not let them diminish my life. Whew, that's a really heavy subject. I say we change topics."

"If you want." His expression had turned thoughtful. Nothing could be dreamier than his blue eyes. He could see right through her barriers to places she liked to keep hidden, which was the last thing she wanted.

Yes, a change of topic was definitely a good idea. An electronic chime chose that moment to fill the air, emanating from Sean's back pocket. Wildflower pricked her ears, listening to the tune, and Eloise patted the mare's neck in reassurance. She wasn't noticing how attractive Sean was as he tugged his cell from his back pocket. A shock of dark hair tumbled into his eyes as he studied the screen. Her fingers itched to brush it back into place.

"A rancher's work is never done," she commented. "Is it your uncle? If you have to head back, I can find home on my own."

"No, that's not it." He hit a button, silencing the phone, and jammed it into his pocket. He didn't sound as breezy as he probably meant to. "Personal."

"Personal? Oh, you so aren't getting away with that." She squinted against the sun as the trail wound due west where light glinted off the wide snake of the river. "Tell me."

"It's nothing." A muscle jumped along his strong jaw line. He shrugged one wide, capable shoulder. "No big deal."

"I know a big deal when I see one." He wasn't fooling her. She'd caught the flash of pain in his soulful blue eyes. The tension ratcheting through him was plain to see. She leaned toward him in the saddle, wanting to reach out and afraid to do so. "Avoiding someone?"

"My ex." He concentrated overly hard on guiding Bandit through the grass.

That was it. No explanation. No elaboration. He turned to marbled stone before her eyes, shutting down, closing up. He was hurting.

Caring poured into her heart, caring she had no right to feel. She brushed a strand of windblown hair out of her eyes, debating what to do. Did she give him his privacy? Or did she express her concern the way any friend would?

"Can I ask why she is calling you?" She tilted toward him, amazed by the display of emotion warring beneath the surface of his set face. He wanted to appear unaffected but that was far from the truth. She read the wince of pain and the shadow of regret. "Didn't she break up with you?"

"This is the second time she's called." Tendons corded in his neck, as if he were holding back pain.

He must have loved her very much. Of course he had, since he'd proposed to the woman. He wasn't like Gerald, who had been able to move on so easily. Sean felt deeply and truly.

How could any woman not have wanted him? Meryl didn't know how blessed she was to have had Sean's love and devotion. Anger speared through her, and she had to look away, take a few deep breaths and focus on the serenity of the daisies dancing in the wild grasses. How could anyone have treated him that way?

"Seems things didn't work out with the dentist, so she's decided to apologize to me." He tried to sound aloof.

He almost pulled it off. She would have believed him if she didn't know him so well. She tried to sound aloof too, as if she wasn't hurting and upset on his behalf. "Apologize? Or do you mean she wants you back?"

As he casually shrugged one brawny shoulder again, an attempt at being aloof, muscles rippled beneath his T-shirt and corded in his neck. Her pulse tripped over itself in the silence. Was he going to forgive the woman? Would he go back to her?

That thought doesn't hurt at all, she told herself, ignoring the arrow of pain burrowing into her. She adjusted the reins and concentrated on getting the sun-warmed leather straps just right between her fingers.

"I don't want her back." Sean broke the silence, resolute. "I don't want to be second-string. Not when it comes to being loved."

Whew, that was a relief. Tension rolled out of her and she almost slumped in the saddle. "I've been there, done that, bought the T-shirt."

"I have that shirt, too. I was a fool letting her dupe me like that. I didn't even realize she was seeing someone else." He tugged his Stetson a notch lower to shade his eyes against the sun, but it also hid the emotions he had to be fighting. "My mom and stepdad have one of the best marriages I've seen. I never really thought about it. All those years growing up and watching them, I just thought that was how relationships went. You got along, you were happy and you put the other person first."

"That was my experience, too." It felt as if they were in sync as they rode the gently sloping hillside together. Copses of cottonwood and groves of pine cast shade here and there and hid them from the houses popping up at the edge of town. "I just assumed any relationship I had would be the same as my parents'."

"That's what I did. I was probably naive, but I couldn't see the little things that were wrong. When I did, I argued them away." He guided his big black horse off the trail, turning onto the residential road. His long, wide shadow fell across her. He cleared his throat, but his emotions lingered in the deep notes of his baritone. "If I'd paid attention, maybe I could have ended things earlier and saved myself a lot of agony. I tried too hard to make it work."

"Me, too." It was really hard to think straight with Sean at her side. She had to resist the pull of his attractiveness. She had to hold down wishes that could not be brought into the light. "There were little things that were off, things I told myself not to be so picky about. Gerald always wanted things his way, he forgot the courteous little touches, he always picked the movie we watched. Now and then I worried I was an afterthought to him."

"You told yourself he was busy or had a lot on his mind or that no one is perfect and that you weren't being accepting enough?"

"Exactly." That was it. "Gerald was good to me, not great, but good. I could explain everything away because of the stress of our constant training and competing. We were world champions. Maintaining our title was hard work and pressure. The excuses I made for him came very easily and I didn't even realize it."

"I understand. Once my eyes were opened, I felt stupid because I settled for so little. I couldn't see her behavior for what it was. She didn't want me to see it, but she was biding her time with me." His voice steeled, rising powerfully above the knell of the horse hooves on the paved street. "When she thought she could do better, she did."

"She could not do better, Sean. Not by a long shot." For all his manly strength, he was as vulnerable at heart as she was. He had been devastated as thoroughly. Heartbreak played no favorites but hurt equally. "You loved her truly."

"I thought so, but now I'm not so sure. If it were true love, then my feelings toward her would never fade. They did." He shrugged, sitting taller in his saddle, his chest up, his shoulders straight, his dignity showing.

She admired him so, so much. She feared she liked him even more.

The leisurely dance of a country sunset was deepening with its last chorus. The underbellies of fluffy, marshmallow clouds blazed with bold purples, pinks and reds. Sunset cast jeweled tones into the light that enveloped them like a sign from above. Tall trees cast long shadows over the land and over the occasional house lining the road. Her driveway came into sight and she sighed with sadness. Their ride was at an end.

She hated drawing Wildflower to a stop. For a while, for the length of the ride, she had been able to forget about the cane tucked into the saddle straps. She dismounted, struggling to keep the smile on her face and to hold on to their moment of closeness. She gripped her cane tightly and handed over the reins to Sean. "Thanks for riding with me home."

"I could have taken you in the truck." He tied a loose knot in the end of the reins and looped them over his saddle horn. "But I thought this would be nicer."

"It was." Nice. That was one word for it. Illuminating was another. She tried with all her strength to keep from feeling a single thing as Sean tipped his hat to her.

"Good night, Eloise. I'll see you." He wheeled the horses around to retrace his trail home, sitting so strong and tall in the saddle he took her breath away. "My horse trailer is ready to roll any time you need it."

"I'm still keeping Cheyenne as an option."

"Funny." He held up one hand, riding away into the shadows and the dying rays of light.

Do not fall, she warned herself. Do not even start to fall for the man. He was certain heartbreak waiting to happen.

Chapter Thirteen

In the heat of the mid-afternoon sun, Frank Granger strolled into the main horse barn, whistling. His sons were busy walking the north herd's fence line checking wire. Autumn and Addy were working horses in the arena; he could hear the faint ring of his daughters' laughter as he ambled down the breezeway. The stalls were empty this time of day, smelling of fresh straw and hay, the horses out grazing in the shade of the cottonwoods. It felt good knowing everything was going fine, his kids had the place running like a top and for the first time in years he had leisure time. May as well make good use of it.

"Got Rogue saddled and ready," Scotty called out, giving the gelding a pat. The ranch hand had been working for the Granger family for too many decades to count. "You've been taking off a lot lately."

"That I have." Rogue gave a deep-throated nicker, one of welcome and friendship. He and Rogue had been together a long time, too. He loved his horse because Rogue didn't toss him the knowing grins everyone else in this town did. Rogue held his tongue and didn't ask questions about a certain lady Frank was seeing. Rogue understood a man liked to keep some things private.

"Going to see Cady again?" Scotty stood there grinning, silvered hair slicked back. He crossed his arms over his barrel chest, expecting a confession that wasn't going to come.

"Thought I'd take Rogue out on the river trail." He untied the rein from the wall ring and stroked Rogue's nose. The gelding leaned in, a whicker rumbling deep in his throat.

"The river trail. That goes all the way to the other side of town." Scotty didn't give up. His grin broadened. "Cady's inn is on the other side of town right along that trail."

"What's your point, Scotty?" He swung into the saddle. With a touch of the reins, Rogue backed and moved into the aisle.

"You're spending a lot of time with that fine lady." Humor twinkled in dark eyes. "When are you gonna get up the gumption and propose to her?"

"Just you mind your own business." Frank laughed, shaking his head. Wasn't that everyone's question these days? "I've been a bachelor a long time. I might just be stringing her along, unable to commit."

"I say it's soon." Scotty, more friend than employee, belted out a laugh. "You've been bitten hard. You're in love with her."

"The better question everyone should be asking is how she feels about me." That concerned him. Heat stained his face as Rogue trotted into the sunny yard. His romance with Cady Winslow was as sweet as could be, but it was hard to know if the hopes taking root in his heart matched hers. He nosed Rogue out of the barn and down the hill.

"Dad, are you going to see Cady?" Addy's singsong alto lilted across the fields where horses grazed. She sat on the back of her dappled mare, ponytail askew and grinning wide. Looked like she'd been racing barrels.

"Where else would he be going?" Autumn sidled the mare she was working on up to the end of the arena, opened up to let in the fresh air and sun. She beamed happiness as she waved. It was good to see his girls on top of the world, Autumn about to be married, Addy home graduated from college. "Have fun! Give Cady a hug from me."

"And from me, too!" Addy chimed in.

"Will do." He held up a hand and kept riding, glad for the expansive distance of the fields because they made a long conversation impossible. Horses looked up from their grazing and whinnied, others bounded across the grass toward him. On his other side the yearling calves bawled and leaned against the wooden fence. Buttercup and her troop joined in.

"No time to chat, ladies," he called out to all the creatures on both sides of the fence. "I'll make it up to you later, promise."

Buttercup mooed as if her heart would break. Jasmine and Daisy joined in, their lows rising above the horses' disapproving neighs. Cheyenne would spoil them appropriately in his stead after her long day at the vet clinic was done. He swelled with pride at his daughter, who was doing so well. Mrs. Gunderson climbed the porch steps with a basket on her hip, done with her work in the garden.

"Looks like it's just you and me for a bit, Rogue."

The gelding answered with an agreeable nicker. Larks sang, robins hopped along searching for an early supper and on the far rise of the hill he caught sight of the faint figures of his sons bent to their work stringing wire. He swelled a little more with pride in his boys, working the land. Justin happily married, Tucker about to become a husband. Life was good.

The Lord had blessed him richly in all his children, no doubt about that.

His phone rang, proof his day was never done. He hoped it wasn't a problem that would pull him back to the ranch. He dug his phone from his pocket and checked the screen. It wasn't work, which puzzled him. "Sandi Walters, what can I do for you?"

"You have the nicest housekeeper, Frank. I just talked with her up at the main house. I invited her to our Bible study at the church on Thursday." Sandi Walters worked at the diner and had always been as friendly as could be to his kids. Hard not to appreciate that, even if she'd always been a tad too friendly to him ever since her divorce.

"It's awful kind of you." He leaned back in his saddle guiding Rogue onto the stretch of the county road. The empty ribbon of blacktop was framed by overgrown grass nodding in the wind. "I'm sure Mrs. G. was glad for the offer."

"She was. Say, the reason I'm calling is about the rumor I've been hearing."

"Which one would that be?"

"That your nephew and the youngest Tipple girl are taking in unwanted horses?"

"For once, a rumor in this town is true." Frank chuckled, relieved he didn't have to try to dodge any rumors about his personal life. "You wouldn't happen to know of a needy horse?"

"I do. Would the kids be interested?"

"I'm sure they would. I'll let Sean know."

"Wonderful. It was good talking with you, Frank. I suppose everything is going well with your family?"

"Just fine. Hope everything is well with yours." Rogue turned down Tucker's dirt access road, already knowing where they were headed. Not much got past that horse. The gelding lifted his head, scenting the air, and swiveled his ears. Sean must be nearby. Rogue was an eavesdropper from way back.

Frank said goodbye, pocketed his phone and patted Rogue's neck. "As you heard, we are on a detour. Sean must be around here somewhere."

The spread Tucker had bought shone like an emerald in the sunshine, green fields, growing crops, reaching trees. A small herd of sheep dotted the hillside like dollops of white fluff. Lambs played tag, running and frolicking under the watchful eyes of their mothers. A figure rose out of the herd and lifted a hand.

Sean. The boy had a way with all creatures, cattle, horses, even sheep. He scribbled on a notebook. Must be updating records now that the lambs were tagged and their inoculations were due. Frank urged Rogue up to the fence line. While Sean hiked across the field, Frank texted him Sandi's number. "Found another horse for Cady's stable," he called out.

"Great." Sean might think he was fooling everyone, but the only one he was fooling was himself. The young man's eyes didn't light up because of a horse. No, a certain young lady had something to do with that. Sean hauled out his phone and glanced at the screen, acting casual, as if the gal was no big deal. "I'll give Eloise a call. She'll be pleased."

"Sure, and it's fortunate you have a horse trailer to help out." He held back any teasing remarks because he knew what it was like to be a man deeply in love.

"Looks like Cady is going to have a full barn if this keeps up."

"This economy has been tough on horses, too." Sean moseyed up to the fence, shoulders wide, unaware of the sheep, Cotton Ball, trailing him. "Do you think Tucker will mind if I take off?"

"No, I'll give him a call for you. You just go with Eloise and rescue that horse. That's important." Frank tipped his hat in farewell and reined Rogue away from the fence. Cotton Ball gave a protesting baaah.

"Then I'd better get my trailer hitched up." Sean probably figured he'd kept the anticipation out of his voice and the twinkle from his eyes, but he would be wrong.

The boy was head over heels. It took someone in the same spot to recognize it. *Lord, please watch over my nephew. He might need a little bit of help.*

Frank shook his head, chuckling to himself as he and Rogue headed in the direction of Cady's inn.

See how he didn't feel a single thing when Eloise breezed into sight? Sean grinned to himself, pleased his strategy was working. He opened the truck door for her as she padded down the inn's front steps, leaning on her cane. He hardly noticed the dip of her gait, for her beauty outshone everything. Her hair was down, unbounded, falling across her slender shoulders like liquid gold. She'd pulled on blue jeans, although she wore a ruffled blouse, which obviously had been meant to go with a classy blazer and a skirt.

"Word is spreading around about your rescue mission." He gripped the door handle tightly as she approached. "Now folks are starting to call us."

"It's Cady and Julianna's rescue mission," she corrected sweetly, bounding past him, and leaving a scent of honeysuckle in the air and a tug on his ironclad heart. "But it is an awesome thing. Cady has a lot of empty stalls to fill."

"How are the horses we've already rescued?" He watched her avoid his attempt to help her as she hopped onto the seat.

"Settling in, improving, eating." When she smiled, she could make him forget every one of his troubles. "They have names. Since Julianna named her favorite one Dusty, Cady is calling the others, Rocky, Clay and Pebbles."

"Funny. Cady has a sense of humor. I'm sure the horses are lapping up all kinds of attention."

"More than they know what to do with. Our employees head to the stable on their breaks, Cook saves carrots and apples to bring out to them and as for Jenny and Julianna, they are majorly attached. They hardly leave the stable. Their father arrived yesterday to take them back home. Apparently he didn't want the girls flying by themselves. They leave tomorrow."

"How is he going to pry the girls away from the horses?"

"I don't know. I wouldn't have the heart."

Speaking of hearts, his was still successfully barricaded. He closed her door and circled around the front of the truck, pleased because he hadn't noticed how lovely she was today, more lovely every time he saw her. He'd hardly glanced at her mouth that looked sugarcookie sweet. Pleased with himself, he yanked open his door and hopped onto the seat. Not a single feeling crept in, other than the cheerful joy lighting up inside him. Joy from taking an afternoon off work, that was the only reason.

"Adam and the girls aren't going to stay for Autumn's wedding?" He put the truck in gear and hit the gas.

"I don't know. We'll see how persuasive Cady and the girls turn out to be." She shrank the passenger compartment, making it seem much smaller than it had been before. Unaware of what she'd done, she clicked her seatbelt. "I do know that Cady saddled up Misty not long ago and left to meet with your uncle."

"Frank was mighty chipper earlier. He's awful serious about your boss."

"What was that? I saw that scowl."

"I was just thinking that he'd been single for so long. I don't know how he can give up his lone-wolf status after all this time."

"Maybe he turned in his membership card?"

"Funny. Or maybe he forgot to pay his annual dues and he got tossed out. He used to be my role model, but now? Not so much." He shook his head, feigning disappointment. The gentle notes of Eloise's laughter didn't touch him. Nothing could. His emotions were stone, his will unbreakable, and if he faltered just a little, he knew he would be in big, big trouble.

"Look, there they are."

Her voice changed, holding a hint of a wish, a touch of a dream and his impenetrable defenses wobbled a tiny bit before he could get them under control. Oblivious, she pointed in the direction of lush green fields and leafy cottonwoods to where the river glinted and two horses stood side by side, their riders holding hands. The tilt of Frank's Stetson, the upturn of Cady's face and the gild of the sun radiated an immeasurable tenderness.

The barriers Sean had up slid right down. Fortunately

he could concentrate on his driving and pretend it hadn't happened.

"It's nice to see Cady so happy." Eloise turned her attention forward, since the speeding truck had left the couple behind. "I think she's been alone for a long time."

"Just like Frank," he said, although that wasn't new information. He couldn't seem to think straight. What he needed was a safe topic of conversation, one that had nothing to do with love or romance or happy couples. "Did you get any information about this horse we're going to see?"

"All I know is that they have a stray horse they don't know what to do with." She settled back against the seat. "Troy sounded busy when I called. You know what ranch work is like."

"I do. It's always something, which is what I like about it." He hit the signal and turned onto the county highway heading north. Town was a distant blur of color as they sailed by. "I'm a temporary hire at the Granger ranch, but I'm hoping I will be so invaluable after Autumn comes back from her honeymoon Uncle Frank will keep me on. It helps that Tucker has moved into his place across the road. There's more acreage and more livestock to tend. Everyone is spread thin."

"Will they be combining the ranches?"

"Looks like it. It will make both spreads easier to run." He eased off the gas and pulled off the highway. "That's a lot of acreage, so I'm hoping it means long-term job security for me. Plus, Autumn might not want to work so many long hours when she's married."

"All excellent news for you. So this means you have a fair chance of sticking around?"

"Just try and get rid of me."

"Good." The effect of the man's dimples could make any girl forget to breathe. It didn't mean a thing that she couldn't draw in air. Any female would naturally feel a little dazzled by his smile.

The wide gravel lane spooled between rows of fence posts and verdant pastures. Cattle lifted their heads from grazing to watch their approach. Calves ran alongside the fence line, kicking up their heels and chasing the truck. Up ahead, a brick ranch house rose into sight. A row of barns and outbuildings marched along the base of the low hill. Sean navigated toward the buildings, bumping along the private drive, hands on the wheel, shoulders wide, simply his ordinary self but he made her rib cage tighten with wishes she could not acknowledge.

"Sean. Eloise!" A man in his thirties looked up from working a horseshoe, released the animal's hoof and stood. "You didn't waste any time gettin' here."

"Cady wanted me to follow up on this right away." She rolled down the window, squinting against the sun. "She's on a mission to save as many horses as she can, for little Julianna's sake."

"So I hear. I applaud it, too." Troy left the horse cross-tied and ambled over to the truck. "Sean, long time no see. It's good of you to lend a trailer to Cady's cause, although I'm bettin' your uncle has something to do with it, huh?"

"Maybe, but that's all I know. I don't have any scoop about his intentions." Sean hopped from the truck.

"Hey, I was only speculating!" Troy chuckled as he opened Eloise's door with a slight squeak, the sound startling her. It took effort to force her gaze away from Sean, tall and muscular, bounding around the front of the truck. Warm air breezed over her and she grabbed her cane.

"Everyone in this town is speculating." Sean still smiled, nothing about him had changed except for a harsh twist in his words. "Since there's no movie theater in these parts, folks have to have something to watch."

"You know it," Troy agreed good-naturedly and held out his callused hand, offering to help her down. His dark gaze lingered on her cane and pity wreathed his features.

Pride kept her from taking his hand. Any moment Sean would march into range and see the expression on Troy's face. Aware of the weakness in her left leg, she eased off the seat and landed on her good leg, dug the tip of her cane into the powder-soft dust coating the driveway and tried to stand straight and strong as if she were fine, just fine.

"I'll get the door," Sean said tersely, which was strange because he was an easygoing guy, but he was definitely ruffled about something. "Where's the horse, Troy?"

"This way." Unconcerned, the cowboy knuckled back his hat and headed in the direction of the nearest gate. A cloud of dust rose with each step. "The poor thing showed up about a few days ago."

It was hard to guess what Sean was thinking. His dimples had faded into a stern frown as he shut the door. He kept at her side, his impressive shadow tumbling over her as they walked together toward the rails. She gripped her cane tight until her knuckles went white, sorely aware that every other step she took was imperfect. What if Sean looked at her the way Troy had? What would it do to her heart if he ever did?

"Come on, girl." Troy chirruped, gesturing toward

a sad-eyed mare who hung back from the rails. "She showed up just hanging around the fields looking in at all the horses safe in the pasture."

"Poor girl." The mare was thin, not emaciated, but lost looking as if she had known too much disappointment in her life. There was no hope in her gaze, no spirit in her stance as she lifted her head to scent them. Wariness haunted her.

"Pretty girl." Sean leaned against the fence, his tenseness faded. "Is she lost?"

"That's what I thought at first," Troy explained. "I brought her in but she doesn't have a microchip or a brand. There's no way to identify her."

"She's a sweet thing." Sean held out his hand, palm up.

"Do you think she was abandoned?" Eloise watched the mare stretch out her neck and creep toward Sean's hand one hesitant step at a time.

"That's my guess," Troy answered. "Folks are pretty vigilant here. A missing animal wouldn't go missing for long so it stands to reason she was probably let go. I think she's put a lot of miles on her hooves. She's walked so far on bad shoes, she could have gone lame."

Another needy creature found just in time. *Thank You, Lord.* Eloise was truly grateful as the cautious mare tentatively brushed her nose against the tip of Sean's fingers and jumped back, as if waiting to see what would happen next.

"Don't worry, sweetheart," he murmured, kindness and warmth layered in his voice, and the mare responded to it. She shook her mane, nickered nervously and reached out again.

"That's a good girl." When he spoke, it was as gently as a man's voice could be. He brushed his fingertips over the velvet curve of the mare's nose with infinite caring. No man could be more gentle. "That's right, I'm not gonna hurt you, beautiful."

Worry slid from big brown eyes as the mare inched closer and offered more of her head. As handsome as Sean was, nothing could be more attractive than his compassion as he befriended the horse.

"You are wanted now," Eloise told the mare quietly and earned a nod of understanding from Sean. Her entire heart seemed to be falling and she could not let it. Somehow she had to find a way to stop it. She could not afford to adore this strong man with a depth of caring and kindness.

I wish, she thought wistfully. I so, so wish. It was too bad some things were never meant to be.

Chapter Fourteen

"My boss put an ad in a few local papers." Troy backed away from the trailer, the mare successfully loaded. "If we get a call about the mare, who should I contact, you or Eloise?"

"Eloise." Sean gritted his teeth. Me, he'd wanted to say, but that made no sense. He couldn't explain why he didn't want Troy to talk to Eloise. The thought made his jaw clench so hard his teeth hurt.

"Yes, or Cady." Eloise folded a windblown lock of hair behind her ear, beautiful as always, possibly more beautiful than the last time he'd looked at her about three seconds ago. "You have my cell number. The inn's number is in the phone book."

"Easy enough." Troy knuckled back his hat and apparently figured he had the right to open the truck door for her since he paraded beside her in that direction.

Wrong. Sean yanked open the door, fighting a wave of red hot, boiling jealousy that flashed into existence with a force that rivaled spontaneous combustion. Jealousy wasn't like him, but he couldn't deny the fact that his entire field of vision flashed crimson as Troy made small talk with Eloise.

"Cady and the girls are going to love the mare." She planted her cane in the dust beside the truck, unaware that she was the reason he couldn't breathe. Troy probably felt the same way and that made the shade of crimson darken.

I'm in big trouble, he thought and stepped around the door to block any attempt by Troy to help her into the cab.

"Then I can stop worrying about that lost little horse," the cowboy drawled. "She's in good hands now. The Lord provides."

I'm not a jealous man, Lord. Prayer seemed the only way to deal with the scalding rise of emotion that rocked through him like a lightning bolt. *Please help.*

No answer came on the gust of warm wind or in the call of larks singing from their perch on the fence rails. He took a shaky breath and the rushing in his ears dulled enough so that he could make out the sound of human conversation. He caught Eloise's elbow and helped her up, although she didn't seem to need it.

He was in a fix. He couldn't breathe, he could barely hear or see. It wasn't as if he was looking for a relationship. He wasn't about to turn in his lone-wolf club card.

"Thanks for coming by, Sean." Troy turned to him, affable as always. "You saved me a trip trailering the mare to the inn."

"It was no problem at all. Thanks for the call." It was a total surprise he sounded normal. As he circled the truck red faded from his vision and the rushing in his ears calmed. He felt completely normal as he dropped behind the wheel.

"Another deserving horse to cherish," Eloise said in her soft, musical alto that made him want to listen forever. "Cady and the girls are going to absolutely adore her. She's just the kind of horse Julianna wanted to save."

"She's a gem," Sean agreed, fairly sure he didn't mean the horse. He could not take his gaze off Eloise as he turned the key and the engine roared to life. Where were his ironclad defenses, the barriers he'd put up, the resolve he'd made not to feel one single thing for the woman?

Gone. They were all gone, as if blown to dust. He didn't know why. He gripped the steering wheel tight and steered the truck back down the driveway, the tires kicking up a thick plume of dust. None of his current feelings were intentional. After his last bout with romance, he wasn't eager to dive back into a relationship. So, what was wrong with him?

"You have saved the day again." Eloise tossed that perfectly sweet smile at him, the one he couldn't resist. The one that played havoc with his heart.

"Hey, all I'm doing is driving."

"Cady and I can count on you, and that means a lot. I wasn't even tempted to call Cheyenne."

"Funny. Frank was quick to let me off work." He couldn't take too much credit. Sure, he wanted to help out as much as the next guy and he cared about animals. He appreciated what Cady was trying to do, but that wasn't the biggest reason he was in this truck with Eloise. Did he want her to know that?

Not a chance.

"I'm going to make a few calls to make sure no one is looking for the mare." She looked relaxed with him, so beautiful he kept forgetting to watch the road.

"Good." The word stuck in his throat—the only word

his brain would produce. His gray matter decided to freeze and he couldn't think of a single thing to say.

Eloise didn't seem to notice. She smiled over at him as the air conditioner carried a hint of her honeysuckle fragrance. Being with her, letting silence fill him, made his soul stir. Emotions threatened to carry him away, but he held fast. He didn't let his heart give a single bump, beat or tumble. He might not be in control of much, but at least he was in command of his feelings and he would stay that way.

"Are you going to the wedding on Saturday?" The words popped out of their own account, as if his brain had decided to ignore his resolve.

"Of course. Do you know anyone who isn't? It's the talk of the town. No one thought Ford Sherman would last as sheriff. No one has stuck around for very long, but he's putting down roots." She adjusted the air-conditioning vent so it blew on her face. "It will be nice to see Autumn happily married. She's waited a long time for true love to find her."

"True." He couldn't deny that. He also couldn't deny the basic truth that love tended to find a person. You could go looking for it, but that didn't mean you could locate it. And if you did, it might not be a love that would be as true or as durable as the one looking to find you.

Maybe that had been his problem with Meryl. He'd wanted to find love. He'd wanted the blessing of it in his life. What he felt for Eloise was different. It was spontaneous and quiet and illuminating, and he couldn't allow himself to acknowledge it, couldn't tumble one tiny bit.

"Things must be getting pretty crazy in your house with all the wedding preparations." She glanced across the fields as he navigated the county road that would bring the inn into sight at any moment. "I imagine there's so many last-minute things that crop up."

"I wouldn't know about that, as I duck my head and try not to listen whenever something comes up." He winked, keeping it light and friendly. "Autumn handles everything well and planning her wedding is no exception. She also has Mrs. G., who is phenomenal. Nothing gets past her."

"Doris is also the best wedding planner in town."

"She's the only wedding planner in town."

"True, but she's also very good." Eloise shrugged, determined not to give in to the wish gathering like a lump behind her ribs. "Autumn deserves a trouble-free day. A perfect day."

"That's what all the fuss has been for," he agreed, keeping his eyes on the road.

"This is making you uncomfortable, isn't it? The confirmed bachelor talking about marriage."

"I'm tough enough to handle it. I think," he added as a quip, using his dimples to his advantage.

If only she were immune. She sighed, unable to stop herself and the wish that could not be buried. Some day, Sean was going to fall head over heels for a woman. He was going to propose to her, marry her, be a fantastic husband to her and raise a family with her. Some woman was going to be greatly blessed to know his kindness, his tenderness, his gentle kiss.

I wish it could be me, she thought. *I wish I could be the one he will love.* Not possible, she knew, as the truck turned into the inn's driveway and the white building with a wide front porch, picture windows and roof gables came into sight between the rustling cottonwoods. Windshields glinted in the sunshine from the guests' cars parked in the lot. Sean kept right, following the trail of blacktop around the gardens to the shining new stable in back.

"Eloise! Eloise!" Julianna came running all in bright pink, from her hair ribbons to her sandals. "Did you bring her? Oh, you did! I can see her through the window."

"We've got her stall all ready." Jenny came at a less enthusiastic jog, but her dark eyes glittered with anticipation. "Aunt Cady put a call in to the vet, and Nate says he is on his way."

"Excellent." It was a relief to hop out of the truck and escape Sean. As much as she cared, it was starting to hurt to be near to him. She welcomed the kiss of the hot sun and the puff of a lazy breeze against her skin. "She is a dear. I think you are both going to love her."

"I love all the horses," Jenny admitted, following her little sister around to the back where the clunk and clatter of the metal ramp going down told her Sean was there. If she listened she could just make out the low murmur of his baritone reassuring the mare.

"Guess what?" Jenny lingered, hands clasped, dark eyes unguarded. "Dad said we could spend the summer here. The whole summer. He's gonna get a house and stay here with us and everything."

"That's great. You seem happy about that."

"I am. I like it here. Julianna does, too. Besides, the horses need us."

"Yes, they do. Very much." There was no doubt the horses had flourished with two little girls to love them. Love makes everything better. Wasn't that one of life's secrets?

Julianna's voice rang like musical chimes, muffled by the trailer. Hooves clomped on the ramp and the little girl raced into sight. "Jenny! Come see her. She's so pretty!"

"Ooh, she's like red velvet."

"She's called a sorrel." Sean strode into sight, leading the horse by a halter and lead rope. The mare stared at Jenny. Sean held the mare capably, crooning to her in reassuring tones and with his easy confidence.

Somehow she had to resist the incredibly powerful pull of gravity on her heart.

I will not fall, she vowed. I won't do it.

"Look, she's taken a liking to you, Jenny." Sean gave the mare her lead and she walked straight to the older girl. Big brown horse eyes gleamed hopefully.

"She's so nice," Jenny breathed, holding out her hands as the mare placed her face in them. "She really does like me."

"Maybe she used to have a girl about your age," Sean suggested as the mare nickered low in her throat, a contented, welcoming sound. Julianna held out her hand to stroke the horse also.

Over the arch of the mare's neck, Sean's gaze found hers. It was more than horses they were rescuing, and she knew by the poignant set of his gaze that he knew it, too. They were repairing wounded hearts and broken promises and giving animals the chance for happiness to find them again.

I cannot fall for him, she told herself, holding on tight with all the strength and willpower she had. She was not in love with Sean. Teetering on the edge, maybe, but she had not made that long, perilous tumble.

Yet.

"Eloise, you brought us another keeper." Cady breezed into sight, the tall solemn figure of the girls' father trailing behind her. "Come, let's show her to her new stall."

Sean handed over the lead to Jenny and stepped away, saying nothing as he backtracked around the truck. It was easy to say goodbye if she didn't look at him. She gripped her cane and headed to the barn, not daring to turn around and wave as he drove away.

Thoughts of Eloise trailed him all the way to the ranch. Images of her burnished by the sun, tenderly petting the new mare, just being Eloise with the air conditioner blowing her hair. He banished them but those images kept coming, impossible to stop. By the time he'd unhitched and hosed out the trailer, he'd lost the battle.

Footsteps knelled behind him when he was winding up the hose.

"Heard Dad took you off sheep duty." Tucker ambled over, dusty from a hard day's work repairing the fence. "Were you able to get the mare?"

"That's an affirmative. She's being properly spoiled in Cady's stables as we speak." He attempted to keep the vision of Eloise from popping into his mind, but it was a half-hearted attempt. He had to accept he had no power when it came to her. Maybe he never truly had. He could see her with the Stone girls, luminous and hopeful as the mare basked in the children's attention.

"Nate's coming over first thing in the morning." Tucker strolled on by with a chuckle. "Earth to Sean. Do you read me?"

"Sorry, guess I'm a little spacey." He shook his head, the understatement of the year.

"Yeah, I remember feeling that way. Still am ever since Sierra and I set a wedding date." There was no disguising the understanding grin one man gave another when he'd been lassoed in by marriage. "There's no way to avoid it now."

"You're doomed, buddy," Sean jested, as it was the lone-wolf way.

Stop thinking of Eloise, he told himself in the silence left behind as Tucker strolled out of sight. Work was done for the day, and he needed to do something to keep his mind from boomeranging back to her.

He hopped in his truck and his phone rang. He whipped it out of his pocket so fast, he didn't even glance at the screen. His palms went damp, his pulse galloped as he imagined Eloise on the other end. "Hello?"

"Sean." A woman's overly bright voice burst across the line.

"Meryl." Shock left him so stunned, he nearly steered right into the fence. His mind spun, too shocked to engage. Utterly blank, he listened to her chatter on.

"I'm so thankful you took my call. Finally. That must mean you listened to my messages. I know you're upset with me, but you took my call." She emphasized the words as if he'd saved the world from a killer asteroid and lived to tell the tale.

His guts clenched. His throat ached. The memory of her betrayal lingered, souring his mouth. "I wouldn't have answered if I had known it was you." He said the truth as gently as he could. "I don't want a second chance with you, Meryl. The first time around was more than enough for me."

"But I made a mistake. You can forgive me, I know you can."

He pulled into his slot in the garage and cut the

engine. Yes, he was capable of forgiveness. "I can't forget and I'm not going to. This really is over."

"I was hoping we could meet. I could drive up your way."

"No. Sorry." He opened the door and let the sweet grass-fed breezes tumble over him, breathed in the fresh air and wide open spaces. The bitterness vanished. He was over her, he realized, thinking over his afternoon with Eloise.

He was losing the battle to deny his feelings. He didn't know how much longer he could hold out.

"You have a nice life, Meryl." He meant it as he hung up, feeling chipper. The tension bunched up behind his rib cage melted away as both boots hit the ground. He jammed his phone into his back pocket, whistling as he crossed the yard and pounded up the porch steps. Buttercup called out, batting her long lashes at him.

"I won't be long, sweetie," he called over his shoulder as he swung open the door. "I'll bring you a treat. How's that, darlin?"

The cow lit up like a puppy at her favorite word, "treat," and did the bovine equivalent of a happy dance.

Female voices rang like music as he kicked off his boots in the mud room. He balked at the circle of women at the kitchen table, most likely busy doing something for tomorrow's wedding. Maybe he could sneak on by before any of them noticed, but Mrs. G. was a sharp tack. She didn't miss much as he padded stealthily into the room.

"There you are." The housekeeper looked up from her place at the table. "Guess you'll be here for supper after all. Frank said not to count on it."

"Uncle Frank doesn't know everything." He tossed her a big grin because he saw her starting to get up.

Probably to fetch him something cold to drink from the fridge. Before he could stop her, one of his cousins did.

"I don't know. Dad is usually right." Cheyenne hopped up instead and circled around the island. "Isn't Eloise with you?"

He saw how deftly she was trying to get information out of him. He wasn't about to be fooled, so he changed the subject. "Shouldn't you be at the vet clinic doctoring animals?"

"Yes, but since my sister is getting married I scheduled the afternoon off." Cheyenne grabbed a trio of pop cans from the fridge. "Don't ignore my question."

"Yeah, we know you're sweet on Eloise." Autumn made a neat little bow out of thin ribbon wrapped like a noose around a bunch of lavender netting. Wedding favors, apparently.

"Ooh, romance." Rori smiled as she leaned back in her chair. "Tell us more."

"I'm down on love, but that doesn't mean I don't want to hear all about it," Addy added.

"Mostly because you're nosey," Cheyenne teased as she distributed the cans.

"Sure. Inquiring minds want to know."

Mrs. G. took a can from Cheyenne, plopped it onto the table and patted an empty chair. "Sean, sit. Make yourself useful. Answer the girls' question."

"You're a romantic, aren't you, Mrs. G.?" He didn't miss trouble gleaming in her eyes. "You were a heartbreaker in your day."

"I still am." She laughed and the kitchen rang with laughter as everyone joined in.

"Maybe we should be talking about your love life, Mrs. G." He plopped into the chair, not complaining as

Addy on his left pushed a mound of ribbons his way and Mrs. G. set her pile of the lavender mesh stuff between them.

"Is it my imagination, or is the boy trying too hard to change the subject?" Mrs. G. asked.

"He's definitely trying to dodge the question," Cheyenne agreed as she wrapped two cookies with care. "That speaks for itself."

"Sure I'm sweet on Eloise. Who wouldn't be? I'm also sweet on all of you and Buttercup." He popped the top on his can and took a gulp of root beer. Good stuff. "Guess what I saw today? Frank and Cady out on a ride together."

"Yeah, we know all about it. If Dad isn't here, where else would he be?" Addy asked with a dimpled grin.

"I'm surprised Cady isn't here helping out." He spread out a piece of the mesh stuff and grabbed two cookies from the bowl. "Isn't this her kind of thing?"

"We wanted to have her here," Autumn explained. "I was going to invite her but then Dad took off to go riding and I thought that was more important."

"Cady's awesome." Addy fussed until she got the bow just right. "I love her. Anyone who makes Dad whistle is primo in my book."

"I can't ever remember him being so happy," Cheyenne agreed as she snapped open her strawberry soda.

"He seems really serious about Cady," Rori said.

"I think he's going to propose." Addy opened her soda. "Can you imagine? After all these years, we'll have a stepmom."

"She will be a great one," Autumn predicted.

"She sent me care packages when I was at school." Cheyenne got busy wrapping up more cookies. "Really nice ones."

"Ooh, me, too." Addy agreed as she lifted her pop can.

"And she emailed me all kinds of encouraging quotes when I was putting in long hours on my rotations."

"I got quotes and nice chatty emails."

"Friendly," Cheyenne agreed. "She didn't have to do that. She was busy getting her inn off the ground, but she took the time to really care."

"That's it. She's genuine. I'm glad Dad has someone like that to care about him." Addy took a sip of her soda. "Ooh, this is fizzy. Cheyenne, did you shake my can?"

"No, but it was tempting."

Laughter filled the kitchen again, the conversation steered well away from Eloise, but that didn't stop him from thinking of her. Knowing she would be at the wedding made him peaceful, as if a great calm were settling inside him. He couldn't wait to see her.

Chapter Fifteen

Maybe she wouldn't run into Sean. Maybe she could safely avoid him. Those thoughts were what got Eloise up the church steps when she wanted to go back to the car. Yesterday's outing with him remained at the forefront of her mind. The million little reasons she cared for him tormented her as she stepped through the doorway and into the sanctuary. Everyone had showed up for Autumn's wedding. The aisles were packed, the pews stirred with folks settling in, visiting, calling out howdy to friends and neighbors.

No sign of Sean anywhere. Major relief. Maybe she could scoot into an aisle and become part of the crowd and when he arrived he would never spot her. Avoiding him was the only plan she could think of to keep her heart safe from the torment troubling her. If she didn't see him, then she didn't have to fight for control of her heart.

"Excuse me, dear." Doris, the minister's wife, bustled by glancing at her watch. She'd been organizing the town's weddings for the last thirty years. She disappeared down the aisle and into a throng of more guests crowding through the doorway.

Eloise gripped her cane and took one step. She didn't get any further before the air changed. She knew he was close even before her gaze found him striding down the lane looking like a Western movie hero come to life in a dark jacket and trousers. All that was missing was his Stetson.

"Eloise." The way his voice warmed around her name made little bubbles pop in her midsection. "I was hoping I might find you here."

Joy inexplicably burst inside her. She tried to stop it, but she couldn't. Her emotions tumbled in a freefall because of the man who strode toward her with his long-legged, confident gait. The afternoon brightened. She became fully alive as if for the first time at his slow, dazzling smile. It was as if she took her first breath.

"I think everyone on this half of the county is here." She feared he could hear the strain in her words. Tension coiled through her, making her feel awkward and anxious.

"The church is packed," he agreed amicably, at ease. "Let's go find a place to sit while we still can. Come sit with me."

Say no, she told herself. Make an excuse. Find Gran. Escape him while you still have your heart. But when he held out one hand in silent invitation, she was helpless to say no. Her hand automatically met his and the drone of conversations faded. At the twine of his fingers through hers, her spirit quieted. Peace permeated her, soul-deep.

Don't start wishing, she thought. Not one wish.

"The house was crazy this morning." Amusement vibrated in the low notes as he shortened his stride to match hers. "There were women, lace, dresses and flowers everywhere before I left. It's too much for a bachelor. I barely survived it."

"You do look worse for the wear," she quipped.

"Thanks. You look amazing."

"Now you are fibbing. You better be careful as you're in a church. Lightning could strike."

"Well, it wouldn't hit me." He'd never seen anything more stunning than Eloise in her summery pink dress. The swingy hem swirled with each step, and her golden hair tumbled in soft bounces to frame her incredible face. She'd blushed at his compliment and the light pink stealing across her nose and cheeks only made her more amazing. He had no clue how she managed to get any more beautiful.

Time to accept he couldn't win the battle. His heart was full of feelings he could not stop.

"What's the latest word on the little mare we rescued?" he asked.

"She settled in just fine. Jenny named her Princess. I think those two are going to be close." She glanced toward the middle of the church. Midway down a row Mrs. Tipple gave him a two thumbs-up.

Poor Mrs. Tipple had way too high an opinion of him. She was the most hopeful one of all. "I'm guessing Nate turned up to give her a good exam?"

"He did. She needed some care, but she will be fine. She needs to be reshod, so the farrier is dropping by on Monday."

"Excellent. While I hope there isn't another horse in need anywhere, if there is we can ride to the rescue. It's been rewarding. I'm glad we're doing this together."

"Me, too." She did her best not to let her adoration show. Tiny wishes kept threatening to rise to the surface that he would look at her and think, wow, and that his feelings were changing, too.

Of course they weren't, but her stubborn hope would not die. No matter how much she knew it had to.

"I need to sit with my family." The words rushed out, more strained than she'd intended. She wanted to come across as unaffected. She wanted to seem like a cool, casual and independent woman who didn't need a man's affections. He would never know how much she wanted him, how he was the man of her dreams.

"Sean, the ceremony is about to start." A man in his sixties moseyed down the aisle, Stetson in hand. "Howdy, Eloise."

"Hi, Scotty. You clean up nice." She'd known the Grangers' ranch hand since she was a small child, although it was rare to see him out of a T-shirt and jeans. "Don't let me keep you. I'm going to sit with Gran."

"Sure." Surprise flashed across Sean's handsome face but it fled quickly. "I'll see you after."

"Sounds great." That came across as breezy and easygoing, didn't it? Pleased with herself, she headed down the row, refusing to give in to the need to glance over her shoulder. She knew better than to fall in love again.

"Hold still, Dad." Cheyenne leaned in to fuss with his tie.

Frank Granger scowled. He wasn't fond of monkey suits, as he called the black tux, but it was his oldest daughter's wedding. He could survive the insult to his rancher's dignity for a few hours.

The room in the church's basement reverberated with excitement. He gazed around, proud of what he saw. His beautiful daughters were dressed up and as grown-up as could be. Maybe it was wishful thinking, but his daughter-in-law, Rori, appeared a bit peaked as she fussed with Addy's hair do. Maybe it was from the excitement, but he suspected it was more than that.

Autumn shone like the happy bride she was, wearing one of her mother's diamond necklaces and decked out in a white lace and pearl dress with some designer label that had taken a chunk out of his savings account—not that he minded. All he'd ever wanted in life was for his children to be happy.

"Doris gave me the two-minute warning." Cady bustled into the room, tall and slender and as pretty as a magazine picture. She was elegance in an understated, dark emerald-green dress to match her eyes and tapped crisply on her coordinating heels. Her soft bouncy locks were tamed into a fancy do that only enhanced the beauty of her oval face. "Are you ready, Autumn?"

"Ready? I was about four minutes ago. Now I'm mostly really nervous. Look, I'm shaking." She held out one hand, which wobbled somewhat terribly.

"Remember how nervous I was when I married your brother?" Rori took Autumn's hand in her own and they leaned together, talking away.

"Ooh, I'm not happy with this," Cheyenne muttered and went to loosen his tie. "Dad, you're not holding still."

"This is good enough. I'm an old man. There's only so much improvement anyone can make with me." He gently tweaked her nose, as he'd used to do when she was small. He could still see her freckles and pigtails, trailing after him when he doctored an animal.

"You aren't so old," Cheyenne quipped gently as she picked a tiny dab of lint off his collar. "Addy! Dad's ready for his picture."

"Ooh, goody!" His littlest bounced up in a swirl of silk, prancing across the room with a contraption in hand. "Dad, you look fab. Gather up, everyone. Group picture!"

It was too late to duck out the door. Cheyenne had a hold on him. That girl wasn't just good at barrel racing and doctoring animals. She was sharp-eyed and she had a strong grip. But he wasn't born yesterday; he knew how to handle a pack of women.

"Addy, give me that camera. I get to do the honors. You all cozy up together so I can get a picture of my girls." He flashed a grin at them because he knew how tough it was for his daughters to say no to his dimples. "C'mon, make your dad happy."

He watched with love in his eyes and a catch in his throat as Rori and Autumn joined Cheyenne and Addy. With the bride in the center and her bridesmaids surrounding her, he positioned his camera. Although his attention was on his girls, he was aware of the other woman in the room, hanging back and quietly watching. Cady had an effect on him, one he couldn't deny. "Alright, big smiles. Say cream cheese."

"Cream cheese," they chorused as he clicked. "Cady! Come join us."

"Oh, no, I couldn't." She was blushing. He forgot anyone else was in the room as she leaned one shoulder against the wall. "I try to avoid cameras at all costs. I take terrible pictures."

"No one here believes that." Autumn floated around him to take Cady by the hand. "I'm the bride. It's my day. You have to indulge me."

"I can't say no to you, sweetie." Cady patted Autumn's cheek. It was a gentle gesture, one of caring that a mother might give a daughter.

His throat tightened up. He knew Autumn and Cady had gotten close over the last year. His daughters pulled Cady into their circle, fussed with her and showed in little ways of tone and gesture that they cared for her. Truly cared. It meant so much to him his vision went a little fuzzy as he snapped the picture. He took a second one just in case. He wanted to make sure to capture this moment in time.

"Calling all bridesmaids!" Doris charged in like a general preparing for a siege. "It's time to go! Follow me. Frank, are you all right? You look a bit overwhelmed."

"I'm the father of the bride. It's my prerogative." He held out Addy's camera, hoping no one noticed he'd managed to avoid getting into the picture.

"Frank." Cady's caring alto and her gentle touch drew his attention. She took the camera before Addy could reclaim it. "Let me take a picture of you and your daughters."

He could read the unspoken understanding in her eyes. She knew what his kids meant to him. He didn't have to say a thing nor did she, but with the comfort of her touch a current zinged between them—a bond of connection and emotion that defied words.

"I've got the music cued, Frank Granger." Doris, whom he'd known since grade school, gave him a scolding look that didn't stymie him any. One flash of his dimples had her reconsidering. "All right, but make it quick, Cady. Autumn, are you ready, honey?"

"Now I am." Her arm hooked into his. Frank gazed down at his little girl and he knew he had to give her away. Not that she was going far. The construction on her house was finished, and it was less than a quarter of a mile from his driveway to hers, proof life was changing. He thanked God for it, but it hurt to know this fork in the road would take her a little away from him.

Cady clicked the shutter, Addy confiscated the camera and Doris steered the bridesmaids out of the room, straightening bows and handing out bouquets as they went.

"This is it, Dad." Autumn's arm tightened in his. "I'm steady now. Whew, glad those nerves are gone."

"Perfectly natural. Same thing happened to me when I married your mom." It was bittersweet to remember that day when his hopes had been sky-high. The road had been tough. In the end Lainie hadn't been a good fit with ranching life, but many of his other hopes had come true. Five perfect children, grown up to be five good people. And as he sensed Cady step from the room to give him and Autumn privacy, he was thankful for a new dream that had come to him in the middle of his life. "Good things are on the way for you and Ford, Autumn. Don't forget. Always be loving and enjoy the journey."

"Thanks, Dad." She went up on tiptoe to kiss his cheek, his sweet little girl.

God was good, he thought as he led her from the room. Never had there been a man more blessed than he.

Eloise stood in the church hall listening to the string quartet. The lilting notes rose over the dozens upon dozens of conversations. So far, she'd succeeded in her latest mission of avoiding Sean at any cost.

"Dad has a hidden ballroom dancing talent. Who knew?" Cheyenne sashayed up in her bridesmaid's dress and doled out the three cups of lime punch she carried. "Look at him go."

"I would give him a perfect ten," Addy declared as she took a sip. She studied her father over the rim of the cup. Frank Granger with Cady in his arms sailed modestly around the dance floor as if all he could see was Cady, as if she were the only person in the entire world.

If only, Eloise wished. She could not hold it back. If only Sean would look at her like that.

"They make a handsome couple." She managed to clear the wistfulness from her voice and took a sip of punch. It rolled over her tongue, sweetly tart. Cady deserved a fine man like Frank Granger. "I'm happy for them."

"We are, too," Addy answered for her sister.

Happy couples were everywhere. Eloise spotted her parents toward the back, waltzing rustily. Silver-haired Hal and Velma Plum waltzed as if they were fifty years younger. The bride and groom gazed into each other's eyes, cocooned in their happiness and love for one another.

"I have to say Autumn and Ford make a beautiful couple," Eloise heard Martha Wisener comment in the crowd behind her. "The town finally found a sheriff who will stay."

"About time, too," Sandi Walters added. "He might be a city boy, but he fits in around here like a stitch in a seam."

"That he does," Arlene Miller concurred.

"Aren't you glad this is not going to happen to us any time soon?" Cheyenne asked with a grin.

"Or ever," Addy concurred. "All that lace and ruffles and being tied down. No thank you."

"Who needs it?" Eloise found herself saying to cover up the sadness of the truth. Romance was not going to find her again. Gerald's words remained like a thorn in her soul she could not pluck out. *No man is going to want that kind of burden. I've tried as hard as I can, and I can't do it. I don't want to marry you now. You're not what you used to be.*

"I am thankful Autumn found a great guy. Those don't come around every day." Cheyenne ran a fingertip along the etched pattern of her glass cup. "They might be much rarer than first thought."

"I'll agree with that." In the crowd, Eloise spotted a familiar shock of dark hair. Wide shoulders. Six-foot-plus height. A dimpled smile and a rugged, handsome face.

Sean. Her pulse screeched to a dead halt. Every neuron she possessed went into a ceasefire. She could only stare, captivated against her will as he moseyed up to Tucker and Owen. Ever since Tucker had proposed to Sierra, her little boy had been glued to his future father's side. It was nice to see the happy child holding on tight and trustingly to the man he clearly adored. Sean lit up as he talked with the little guy. He knelt so he was eye-to-eye with the child, his masculine strength and kindness the most attractive thing she'd ever seen. She caught the word "horse," and "Bandit," so she didn't have to wonder about the topic of conversation.

He would make a good dad. That realization sailed right past her defenses, another wish she could not give voice to. Good men might be rare but they were out there. Sean was the best of the best. She tamped down the dream before it took form. Whatever God had in store for Sean's future, one thing was for certain. She could not be a part of it. She breathed slowly, carefully past the knot of pain behind her ribs and took another sip of punch.

"I never thought the day would come," Martha spoke up again. "Frank has chosen a bride."

"Oh, they aren't engaged so soon, are they?" Sandi Walters commented. "I'm never going to get over the fact that he didn't choose me."

"Me, either. My heart is forever broken," Arlene Miller agreed. It was no secret to anyone the two middle-aged women had been holding out hopes for Frank's interest over the years, but it had never happened. "I keep praying and praying for a handsome widower to move to town. But so far, God hasn't seen fit to answer that prayer."

"It sounds like a good one to me. I wonder what the holdup is?" Sandi quipped.

"Ooh, look who's coming this way." Addy leaned close. "He doesn't seem to be looking at either one of us, Cheyenne."

"No, I think you're right. He seems awful focused on someone else. I wonder why?"

"Ooh, romance." Addy grinned. "I'm all for it, as long as that dreaded disease doesn't come my way."

Eloise swallowed, unable to speak. The sisters' conversation faded, drowned out by the mad drumming of her pulse pounding in her ears. Her neurons began to fire again, but the rest of the world was fuzzy. Only Sean was clear as he shouldered his way closer. Be still my heart, she pleaded.

It was already too late.

"Looks like I've found the prettiest girls in the room." His easygoing charm was turned up to full wattage.

"What did I just say about great guys being hard to find?" Cheyenne teased.

"I can't win with you two." He grinned, unthwarted. "Eloise. I was hoping you wanted to grab some fresh air with me. I've had about all the wedding festivities that a lone wolf like me can stand."

"A lone wolf?" Addy laughed at that. "Try again, Sean. Eloise, we'll see you later."

"I don't even get to say no?" she protested as Cheyenne plucked the nearly empty punch cup out of her hand and Addy spun away on her heels.

"I'm not sure they agree with the whole lone-wolf thing." He shook his head and nodded toward the open doors nearby, where green leaves rustled and a patch of blue sky beckoned.

"You can try to be something you're not, but it doesn't always work out." Her tone remained light. Golden hair tumbled forward like a curtain, shielding her.

"You're right." He agreed, shoving his hands in his pockets, determined to stay casual. "I'm not a loner type. I would like to be, but I may have to admit defeat."

"You can only be yourself." She led the way into the bright fall of sunlight searing the steps. He'd never recalled a time when the green had been greener. The deep verdant color hurt his eyes. The sky burned a bright robin's-egg blue, so stunning the only thing rivaling it was Eloise in her light pink dress, the hem swinging knee length, making her look like a little piece of cotton candy. Nothing on this earth could be sweeter.

He may as well face it. He'd failed because of her. He hadn't been able to wall off his heart or keep himself from tumbling head over heels.

"You are right." He let humor sound in his words but he kept back other emotions. Ones that he might not be ready for, but they came anyway as purely and truly as a Sunday morning hymn. The musical sweetness enveloped him, leaving him forever changed. Tenderness rolled through in persistent and powerful waves, drawing him inexorably closer to a truth he had to confront. "It's time to face the truth."

"What truth?" She curled a strand of hair behind her ear, deliberately avoiding his gaze.

"There's something I've been fighting. I've tried to forget it, ignore it, deny it and it hasn't worked." He drew her to a stop with a hand on her arm.

"What do you mean?" Nerves quaked through her and a spike of fear she couldn't explain stabbed at her chest.

"I know you have said you aren't ready for this, but I want to talk with you." His amazing blue eyes darkened, so deep they revealed his heart. "We have been spending a lot of time together lately."

"We have. It's been nice." What she saw in him made her palms go damp. The nerves quaking through her turned into tremors.

"Nice?" He shook his head. "No, it's been more than that. Being with you has changed me."

"For the better, I hope. Isn't that a sign of a good friendship?" Keep it breezy, she told herself. He didn't ever need to know how much the word "friendship" hurt. He didn't need to know how much she wanted the affection she saw in his heart.

"Friendship, sure." He nodded, no longer easygoing as everything about him became serious. "It's turned into something more. My feelings for you have deepened. I'm hoping yours have, too."

How was she going to stay in denial now? Air hitched in her throat as he leaned closer. The nerves tremoring through her became a full-fledged earthquake as his gaze focused on her mouth. No, she thought, don't give in. Hold on to the denial.

"We agreed on friendship, Sean." She gasped for breath, taking a rapid step back. "That's all it can ever be."

"It's true. I've been fighting it for so long. I've come up with all kinds of excuses but none of it is the truth. It's time to be honest, Eloise, both of us. I can't help how I feel."

"Sean, I am definitely not ready. I'm not going to be. Ever." How could he do this? His feelings may have changed, but they couldn't last. She gripped her cane tighter, feeling wrenched apart. In front of her was everything she wanted and everything that she couldn't have.

"I don't want to look back in life and wonder, what if?" He brushed the pad of his thumb against her silken cheek. "I don't want to stay silent and think about what my life would have been like if only I'd had the courage to speak my heart."

"Sean, this has to stop." Pain laced her plea. "Please."

Didn't she see? From the moment he'd spotted her at the drive-in with his ice-cream cone, he'd been caught like a fish on a hook doing everything possible to try to get away. But watching Autumn pledge her love to Ford made him realize how deeply he felt about Eloise. To have and to hold, in sickness and in health, through good times and bad. That was how he loved Eloise. With all he had, with everything he was, and he could not get the images of the future he wanted out of his mind, images that came from his soul.

"Don't push me away, not again. Not this time. Please." He brushed at the fine, flyaway strands of hair stirred across her face by the wind. "Let me show you how I feel."

"Sean, I—"

"Just close your eyes." Tenderness rose within him like a summer's dawn, gentle and cozy and certain. There would be no going back and he didn't want to. As he cupped her face with his hands, devotion shimmered within him like the rarest of gems, perfect and flawless and valuable beyond all measure.

The images began to unfurl. He saw sunny summer days and cheerful banter over the supper table with Eloise. He saw weekend horse rides, ice-cream cones at the drive-in, a ring on her finger and a baby cuddled in the crook of her arm. He envisioned everything when he gazed upon her. His hopes, his happiness, his dreams. This was what he wanted her to feel in his kiss as he slanted his lips over hers and opened his heart.

Chapter Sixteen

Panic rattled through Eloise's system, but she hadn't believed it was real until his mouth captured hers. Time stood still, their surroundings vanished and there was only the tender, reverent brush of his lips to hers. Her pulse halted, her soul stilled and she prayed the moment would never end.

It was perfection. Never had there been such a kiss. Fairy tales ended with kisses like this. All the wishes she had fought against rose as if they had sprouted wings. Affection welled up through her, affection she'd tried to banish, but hadn't been strong enough to. Love ebbed into her and she reached out to lay both hands against his chest.

For one breathless moment, she had the dream. A fairy-tale ending could be hers. It was just a breath away. Then the metallic clink of a cane striking the concrete shattered the moment and reality rushed in. The dream vanished. She opened her eyes, back to herself, and broke the kiss. Sean's poignant gaze searched hers.

For one blissful minute she'd forgotten who she was. The cane lying at her feet reminded her.

It would always remind her. The joy ebbed away. The hopes uplifting her now gently lowered her back to the ground. The happy-ending wishes evaporated like mist in a wind, leaving her with a reality that she could not dream away.

"That was some kiss." He cradled her face in his hands with infinite tenderness. She wanted his tenderness more than anything. Sincere affection transformed him. He seemed taller, a bigger man in her view. The corners of his mouth hooked into a quiet grin. "I say we do that again."

"You, sir, have an inflated opinion on your kissing ability." She had to let go of the moment. She had to step away from the closeness and she had to end things, but the very essence of her being wanted to hold on, to keep dreaming, to never let him go. "It was a perfectly adequate kiss."

"Adequate?" Humor danced in his tender blue eyes. Affection warmed the low notes of his voice. "That kiss was a good deal more than adequate. I'm a great kisser."

"I'm not exactly sure where you got that idea." She smiled, fighting to keep things light but the grief inside her began to grow. She could not stop it. It wrapped around her in icy swirls.

"I'm apparently misinformed. That means only one thing." Unaware, Sean gazed at her with honest love, tall and stalwart and everything, just everything. She wanted his love so much, but her injury was a burden. He leaned in, his fingers feather-light against her chin. "Practice makes perfect. I'm going to need a volunteer to practice on. Interested in the job?"

"That sounds like cruel and unusual punishment to me." Just a little longer, she hoped. Maybe she could hold on to the gift of being close to him, laughing with him, just a little longer. She drew in a shaky breath, straightened her shoulders and grabbed hold so very hard to the moment. "You might have to find someone else."

"Sadly, there have been no other takers. I can't think why." Gentle amusement stretched his kissable mouth, softening the lean lines of his face. A face she could gaze on forever and never get her fill. A face she would never forget through the years. He leaned in closer still. "Are you ready for kiss number two?"

Yes, her heart answered. No, her common sense insisted. No. Misery pulled her down and she felt smaller, shorter, diminished. Unable to hold on, the dream slipped through her fingers. This perfect moment shattered and time rolled forward again. She could not deny the past or wish foolishly for the future that the accident had taken from her. Gerald's words rolled into her mind, no matter how hard she tried to stop them. *No one wants a burden for a wife. No man can take that long-term liability. It's too much sadness.*

She steeled her spine and took a step back. She had to do the right thing. She had to be realistic.

"No more kisses, Sean." She hated the shock that swept across him. He stared at her for a moment, blinking, as if not sure he had heard her correctly. His brows arched in confusion. Crinkles dug into the corners of his eyes in bewilderment.

"I hadn't thought. You're right." He glanced slowly from side to side. A soccer ball rolled with two grade school kids in pursuit. "This is a public place."

"A really public place," she agreed.

"What we feel for one another is private. Just between you and me." The tenderness within him deepened with a strength he'd never known before. It bound him to her with a steadfast connection that would never break. "Why don't we take off? Autumn is happily married, they are about to leave for the airport at any minute. No one will miss us if we don't stay for the send off."

"I can't go with you, Sean." Her words were heavy with sadness. "That kiss was wonderful, but it never should have happened."

"Shouldn't have happened? I don't understand." He couldn't wrap his mind around it. Maybe because he didn't want to. The depth of devotion he felt for her was greater than anything he'd known before. How could something this powerful be one-sided? Didn't she feel the same way, swept up by feelings too amazing to deny?

"I shouldn't have let you kiss me," she confessed. "I should have stopped you."

"Just like last time?"

"Yes." She sounded as though she were strangling, as if she were breaking apart from the inside out, just like he was. "This is all my fault. I shouldn't have let it happen."

"What do you mean? You kissed me back. I felt it. I know this is right." He raked a hand through his windblown hair, frustrated. "I am in love with you, Eloise. More than I ever thought possible."

"Maybe you just think so." Didn't he know how his words were tearing her apart? With as much dignity as she could summon, she knelt to retrieve her cane. "You called off a wedding. Seeing Autumn get married today affected you."

"Sure it did. I was happy for her." He straightened his spine, drawing himself up taller than ever. "The past is over. I've dealt with it. You are the one who affects me. Just you, Eloise."

She barricaded her heart so those marvelous words would not penetrate. He really meant it. He loved her. She took a step back, holding her cane so tight because her knees went shaky. His love was the one thing she wanted above all else and the one thing she couldn't have. Agony sliced through her like a sharpened blade. Her dear, sweet Sean. He'd done what she hadn't thought was possible. A man had fallen for her, cane and all.

But it couldn't last. She knew better than to believe.

"This is the part where you say, 'I love you too, Sean.'" He swallowed hard, tension bunching along his jawline. He towered over her, magnificent and vulnerable. He was all she could ever want, her most cherished of dreams, a prayer she dared not ask for.

"I can't." Tears pricked behind her eyes. She would give anything to simply savor this precious moment, forget the past and lay her cheek against the unyielding plane of his chest. To know what it would be like to be enfolded in his strong arms and to feel the beauty of his love.

But she had been down this road before. She didn't want to hurt him, but she had to be honest. He deserved no less.

"Sure you can," he persisted, fighting pain that crept across his face and cut grooves around his failing smile. "You might add how you didn't expect to feel this way for me, too. It's overwhelmed you but it's everything you want."

"I wish." She wanted that more than her very breath. The words stuck on her tongue, the ones that would drive them apart forever.

"Then we don't have a problem." His smile won out, driving away his hurt. Nothing was more dear to her than a loving smile on his face, than the amazing truth of his devotion twinkling like a promise in his eyes. "Now, about that kiss."

"There can't be another." How could she end this, if there was? No, she had to hold on to her resolve. She gripped her cane tightly, drawing herself up as straight as she could.

Lord help me, please. Help me to do this the right way. She swallowed hard. Hurting Sean was the one thing she'd never meant to do. The notes of the string quartet wafted on the wind, the faint drone and laughter from the church hall, the merry sounds of a wedding party all reminded her of what she could never have.

"Sure we can kiss again. It's entirely possible." He winced, as if he were in pain, but he was stubborn. He didn't want to let go either. "You just lean in, close your eyes and we kiss. It's that simple."

She wanted to fight for him. If she did as he asked, if she accepted his kiss and grabbed the wonderful lifeline of the love he offered her, then what would happen? What would their future be?

She knew the outcome. She'd already lived it. She knew how hard he would try to love her over time, as her disability became a bigger and bigger issue between them. How could she hold a man like him? He was outdoorsy, he was always on the move, he lived a physically active lifestyle. His precious love for her would fade and so would the amazing love in his eyes when he looked at her.

How could she survive that? Imagining it crushed her as if an essential part of her was dying. Ending this now was the only choice for either of them. If she rejected him now, one day he would have the happy future he deserved with someone whole, with someone who would never let him down.

"I don't want another kiss." The words felt torn from her, leaving her raw and bleeding. She could not endure the flash of agony darkening his gaze. "Trust me, you feel this way now but over time that will change."

"Impossible. My love for you will never fade, never alter, never diminish." So sincere. He braced his feet, mighty shoulders squared, looking like a Western hero to whom legends could never do justice. He was bigger than life and genuine to the core, everything she'd ever wanted, every dream she'd ever had.

Everything she had to walk away from.

"You say that now. You have the best intentions. But this is for the best." She leaned on her cane and backed down the sidewalk. "From now on, I'm going to have Cheyenne help me with any horses that need rescuing."

"Don't do this, Eloise." He clenched his jaw until it hurt, until tendons stood out on his neck. "At least give us a chance."

"I can't." Tears swam in her eyes but didn't fall. The silent plea pinched her lovely face. Silently, she begged him to understand. She wanted him to let her go.

"Goodbye." She choked on the word. Misery wreathed her features as she spun around, tapping down the sidewalk away from him with great determination. As if she could not get away from him fast enough.

Crushing pain left him in tatters.

"At least tell me why." His call echoed down the sidewalk and she stiffened. Her shoulders straightened. She stopped, clutching her cane. The wind swirled the hem of her skirt around her slim knees and ruffled the straight fall of her glossy blond hair. Alone, a solitary figure on the empty sidewalk, she broke his heart. The pain he felt was nothing compared to hers.

"Why do you think this can't last?" He jogged to catch up with her. She could end this, push him away, never want to see him again, and all the resulting pain would be nothing compared to the torture of knowing she was hurting.

"You know why." She kept walking, the tap of her cane counterpoint to the strike of her low heels on the concrete.

"I'm a man. I don't know anything." Humor had always worked with her in the past. "You have to clue me in."

"Look at me." She tapped faster, chin up, jaw set, so tense she looked fragile, as if she were holding herself so tight because she was ready to crack apart. She might think she was hiding her despair, but not from him. Never from him.

Tenderness deepened, becoming impossibly profound. In all the world, nothing could matter more to him than her. "I'm looking. I see a beautiful woman who has made me fall in love with her."

"I made you?" She stopped, faced him, her eyes dark with sorrow. "I did no such thing."

"Yes, you are completely to blame." He brushed windswept bangs from her eyes, moving in close because he could not stay away. "You captivated me right from the moment I saw you at the drive-in. Then you roped me into helping you with the horses, and I was a goner. The least you can do is tell me why I'm not good enough for you."

"Not good enough?" Her face twisted. Concern for

him layered her voice. "You are entirely too good. Don't you see? The problem is me."

"How could you be a problem, darlin'?" He'd never seen anyone look so defeated, as if the sun would never shine again. His soul buckled and he fell harder, loving her more. Maybe he'd been so busy trying to be a lone wolf protecting himself he hadn't realized that she had been doing the same. "Maybe now is a good time to let me know. So I can understand why you have shattered my heart."

"Oh, Sean, you already know the answer." Tears pooled in her eyes, but they didn't fall. Tears for him, he realized. "It's because of this."

She tapped her cane.

"I told you, I don't see that. Eloise, I only see you."

"Yes, but you said that as a friend." A friend was different from a boyfriend. She'd learned this the hard way.

"I mean it always." Stalwart, that was Sean.

He didn't know the truth about her injury. What if she leaned on him, opened her heart without reservation and gave him all the trust and devotion she possessed? All she could see were her fears that Gerald had been right. No man was going to love her enough to stay. She squeezed out the images of Sean growing tired of the challenges, of Sean leaving her for someone else, of Sean breaking her heart.

Too late for that. She was already shattered. She had to tell him the whole story.

"I remember the exact moment when Gerald fell out of love with me." She hated the tremulous sound in her voice and the catch in her throat that she could not swallow or clear away. "It was when he came to visit me at the hospital as he'd been doing faithfully, but it was the first time he'd seen me using a wheelchair."

"You were in a—?" He didn't finish. He looked startled.

She nodded. Here was where Sean would see her differently. She straightened her spine, steeling herself for it. It had to be done. He deserved to know why. He would want to end this.

"For how long?" he asked.

"Six months. They were the hardest of my life." She could not bear to watch the caring slide from his gaze, so she stared at the sidewalk ahead. She caught a glimpse of the main street and the Steer In, where the lot was empty. The bright sun tumbled over her with summer's heat and light, but she felt locked in the shadows of the past. "Don't get me wrong. I was deeply thankful to have survived the car accident. When I was trapped in the driver's seat, terrified and unable to move, I thought I might die there. I thought it was the end."

"I'm sorry you had to go through that." Sympathy layered his words. He didn't sound distant, as if he was emotionally withdrawing yet, but it would come. She had to prepare for it.

"So I tried to be positive when they told me my spinal cord injury was complete and permanent and I would never walk again. I fought hard, and I walked again." She pushed away the crushing grief that had consumed her at the time and that was consuming her now.

"But you were in a wheelchair for a while," he empathized.

"Yes." The lazy summer breeze rustled through the leaves of the trees marching alongside the curb, and the world so bright and colorful and summery made her want to believe that a man's love might be strong enough to accept all her imperfections.

Except she knew better.

"There's no guarantee the paralysis won't be harder to compensate for as I get older." She squared her shoulders, ready for the rejection she knew was coming. She'd known it from the moment she'd met Sean and been attracted to him. She had plenty of experience with this moment, thanks to her grandmother's fix-ups. "Over time, it is likely I may be a paraplegic again."

"I see."

No man, not even Sean, could love her now.

She did her best not to let it show as she took a wobbly step forward. Her knees were far from steady. Any moment he would turn away. Since it was Sean, he would be kind, gallant, gentlemanly, but he would not look at her with love in his eyes. Never again.

"This was the biggest reason behind your breakup with Gerald?" He dug his fists into his pockets. "He bailed on you when you were injured?"

"He was a nice guy. He wanted to do the right thing. He wanted to behave the right way. He tried to be there for me, but it was hard. When I was in the hospital, the prognosis was so grim. When I was in a wheelchair, there were a lot of adjustments to get used to. There were logistical challenges like sidewalks and finding the wheelchair-accessible ramps instead of stairs, which is harder than you think. So much had changed between us, I had lost so much. The sadness was simply overwhelming." She bowed her head, her hair cascading forward to hide her face. Now he knew the truth. He was free to go. He would be polite, he would be sympathetic, but he would leave.

"You said there were other things wrong with the

relationship." He watched her carefully. His gaze had darkened, his forehead furrowed with thought.

"Yes. Our relationship wasn't as solid as it should have been, but nothing could have withstood the strain. Sometimes love isn't enough."

"Sometimes." He had to agree with that. But at least now he knew what had wounded Eloise so badly she had lost her faith in the fairy tale. He had, too, until she saved his heart. "You would be worth all of that and more. My love for you is strong enough."

"What did you say?" She gazed up at him, disbelieving.

"I love you now, I'll love you then, I'll love you forever. No matter what." He towered over her, more breathtaking than any hero could possibly be. "Nothing is ever going to change that."

No, it couldn't be true. She felt wrenched into pieces, wanting to believe. He was being chivalrous. Optimistic. He was such a good man, he was saying what he wanted to be true instead of what actually was.

"Love is kind." As if he sensed her reluctance, he bridged the distance between them and cradled her chin in his hands. *Love bears all things, believes all things, hopes all things, endures all things. Love never fails.*

"First Corinthians." How could she not recognize those words? They stirred her soul and lifted her hopes, but how could she believe? She had been through sadness and loss and had worked hard to rebuild her life realistically, so she could never be hurt like that again. How could she be sure?

The truth was in Sean's eyes. He gazed at her with endless, abiding love, more powerful than it had been before he'd known about her prognosis. He knew the whole truth and he loved her more.

Joy rolled through her like a prayer answered and she leaned into his touch, savoring the warmth of his fingertips against her face, the bliss of this moment, knowing she was truly loved.

"Now that I've bared my soul, that only leaves one question." Vulnerability flashed across his rugged features. "How do you feel about me?"

She laid her hand on his chest, remembering how gentle he'd been with the mare. How good he was to all God's creatures. He would never hurt anyone intentionally. He was one man who would always cherish her.

I love him, she finally admitted. I truly love him.

When his hand cupped her chin, she went up on tiptoe. His lips brushed hers with a beauty that brought tears to her eyes. She hated for it to end. Sean must have felt the same way because his hand lingered against her jaw and his gaze locked with hers. It was like being soul-to-soul.

"I love you with the kind of love that never fails." Love sailed through her so forcefully, it nearly lifted her from the ground. Bliss drove out all doubt as she wrapped her arms around Sean, her Sean. Being enfolded against him was the sweetest blessing, the only one she could ever want. Dreams she thought long lost burned as bright as the sun. There was so much good ahead in store for her life she could not hold the images back—glimpses of Sean proposing on bended knee, a wedding in the town church, a little home made happy with their lasting love. So very much good ahead, she held him more tightly, determined never to let go.

"There is one more thing we have to talk about." Sean stepped back just enough to meet her gaze. "I would like to discuss the possibility of more kisses."

"I would be in favor of it."

"Good, then we are in perfect agreement." He claimed her lips in a kiss that dimmed the sun with its beauty and captured her soul with its sweetness.

Romance had found her, after all.

Epilogue

"Do you know what your problem is, Eloise?"

"I didn't know I had a problem, Gran." Eloise adjusted her cell phone against her ear as she reined Pixie off the country road and onto Main. Town was busy for a hot June Saturday afternoon. A couple of vehicles were parked in front of the diner, she recognized a Granger pickup, and a truck or two at the feed store. Yep, there was nothing like small-town living. Enjoying the peace, she lifted her face and let the temperate winds puff her bangs off her forehead. "My life is nothing but blue skies. Not a cloud in sight."

"You spend way too much time helping in my garden instead of with that young man of yours. Next time you come over to weed, you bring along young Mr. Granger."

"I might consider it."

"I'll make him some of my homemade lemonade. I'm pleased you found Mr. Right, but I'm bummed I didn't find him for you."

"Yes, sadly my blind-date fix-ups have come to an end. Forever." Hallelujah. That wasn't the greatest thing about being with Sean, but it was a definite perk. She'd found the best man, the very best. "Now that my blind-date days are over, whatever will you do to amuse yourself?"

"You need to ask? I've already got your wedding figured out. The minute he pops the question, you let me know. I've got a notebook started and the church hall booked."

"Help me, Lord." She sent the prayer heavenward. Was her grandmother ever going to stop meddling? Not that she minded, but it was the principle.

"I just want you to be happy, sweet pea."

"I want that for you, too." She so loved her grandmother. Pixie lifted her head, neighing in welcome at the sight of the black gelding standing in the drive-in lot where a car should be parked. Bandit lifted his nose in an answering welcome, and a cowboy moseyed into sight.

Handsome.

"Gran? I've got to go."

"All right, dear. I'll see you this evening. Don't forget to bring that boyfriend of yours."

"I'm making no promises." She didn't remember disconnecting the call or stuffing the cell into her pocket. The man beside his horse with a Stetson shading the splendor of his face commanded every shred of her attention.

"Hey there, pretty lady." He tipped his hat, his deep baritone layered with warmth and humor. "How would you like to join me for an ice-cream cone?"

"I could be tempted." The strong, lean lines of his cheekbones, his sparkling blue eyes and his chiseled jaw held her captive. Wow. "What is a handsome man like you doing here all alone?"

"Trying to pick up a gorgeous chick." Humor flashed in his bright blue gaze. "Interested?"

"Very." She slipped off the saddle and into his waiting arms, such strong arms. There was no place on earth she would rather be than enfolded against his chest, so near to him their souls felt as one.

His chin rested on the top of her head as she snuggled closer and cozy feelings left her smiling into his sun-warmed T-shirt. He smelled like summer and hay and leather. She never wanted to let go. If she could stay just like this cuddled in Sean's strength, she would ask for nothing more.

"Guess what I did today?" His lips brushed her hair.

"Did you end up going to the sale with your uncle?"

"Sure did. I tagged along at the auction over in Sunshine. The ranch did real well selling off some of the cattle." He paused, remembering. He was a permanent employee now and the excitement of the bidding, all the cows to check out and spending time with his uncle and cousins had been fun. But it wasn't the highlight of his day. "Frank came on an errand with me to offer his opinion."

"An errand? You didn't say anything about that before."

She leaned back in his arms, so lovely she knocked the air from his lungs, so beautiful his spirit ached with adoration. Spending time with her and opening his heart to her had been the greatest reward of his life. He was no lone wolf, never had been. He could admit it. He was a pack man, a family man, and he was proud of it. He thanked God daily for the blessing of Eloise in his life.

"It was a top-secret mission." In the bold summer

sunshine he saw another piece of his future. A little tod-
dler clinging to her knee and a new baby in her arms.
Birthdays, holidays, anniversaries spent with her, years
rolling by, each one better than the last. A sense of
rightness filled him up until his vision blurred and all
he could see was her, Eloise, the reason for his life.

"Ooh, sounds mysterious. Top secret." She dazzled,
from the inside out. "Don't tell me you made a stop at
your favorite pizza place and didn't bring home any leftovers for me?"

"No pizza, no leftovers. It wasn't that kind of mission." Behind him he heard Bandit snort his opinion, as
if he disapproved of the place and time, but Sean could
not wait. Love overwhelmed him and his decision was
made. Pixie nodded at him, as if she were saying to go
for it. So, he did.

He tugged the ring out of his pocket. The gold band
gleamed warmly in the light. The square-cut diamond
framed by emeralds winked like a promise made to be
kept. His entire spirit stilled with the importance of the
moment.

"I was going to do this tonight at sunset in a field of
wildflowers," he confessed. "I hope you don't mind we
are in a parking lot, but where I am standing is where I
first was bedazzled by you."

"That's an engagement ring." She stared wide-
eyed, surprise on her dear face. "That was your secret
errand?"

"Yes. The diamond is forever, the emeralds are because they match your eyes, which are now my favorite color. You are my favorite gal." He took in a shaky
breath. Worry crinkled his forehead. Love warmed his
voice, so much love. "Do you know what I see when I
look at you? A porch."

"A porch?" Fine, not what she was expecting but the adoration on his face made her pulse skip three beats. Anticipation left her breathless. "Why a porch?"

"Because on that porch I see a gray-haired couple sitting side by side on a porch swing, holding hands."

"Are they watching the evening unfold?"

"Yes. They do that every warm summer evening, just as they've done every year of their married life. They are happy together." He towered over her, stalwart and incredible and true. "You can tell how much the man adores his wife every time he looks at her."

"That couple is us?" she asked, her eyes growing watery.

"Yes." His eyes deepened with emotion as he cradled her hand in his. Such a gentle touch. "That is what I see when I look at you. I want to marry you. I want to raise a family with you. I want us to be that silver-haired couple happy with a life well spent adoring one another through thick and thin. With every day that passes, I promise to cherish you more. Please marry me, Eloise. I love you so much."

"Not more than I love you." How could she say no to that? It was every dream she'd lost, everything she'd ever wanted with the one man she treasured above all. The sun chose that moment to brighten, as if heaven were trying to spotlight the moment. She realized this is where God had been leading her all along, that He had given her more than the accident had taken away.

"Y-yes." Happiness made the word stutter like a sob in her throat. Tears filled her eyes, and she blinked hard. Joy was too small of a word to describe her feelings. "I want to marry you more than anything and spend all my days loving you. It's a fairy-tale ending."

"This isn't an ending. It's a beginning."

"The best beginning."

He slid the ring on her hand and his gaze locked with hers. She felt the impact all the way to her soul. She twined her hand with his, overwhelmed with emotion. Their hearts, now in synchrony, beat as one and always would. Their bond was unbreakable and everlasting.

"Hey, Eloise! Hey, Sean." Chloe clumped up on her skates, carrying two ice-cream cones. "I was right! You guys *were* dating. Now you're engaged. I *so* called it. Hey, a guy was just in for lunch. He's from the next town over and he asked me if the inn was still taking in horses. Are you?"

"Absolutely."

"I have an address. I'll get it." Chloe thumped off, her skates clumping on the blacktop.

Eloise saw the spark of happiness in Sean's eyes as the sunlight caught the diamond on her left hand. Life was good, so very good. "Can you believe it? More horses to rescue."

"Looks like our mission continues, gorgeous." He knelt to boost her into the saddle. "Let's go."

* * * * *

Dear Reader,

Welcome back to Wild Horse, Wyoming. I hope you have been enjoying the Granger Family Ranch stories as much as I have loved writing them. This time cousin Sean has hired on at the ranch to help out. He is recovering from a broken engagement and has decided that no woman is ever going to threaten his lone-wolf status again. Until he meets Eloise, who is in need of a horse trailer, and he can't say no to helping her. While the two of them rescue homeless horses, what are the chances that God will rescue their hearts, too?

In these pages, I hope you have fun visiting returning characters, both human and animal, and lose yourself in a small-town rural way of life. Once again I have tucked favorite things from my childhood into this story—leisurely horse rides, pet cows and chocolate ice-cream cones—and I hope you are reminded of some of the golden memories from your childhood. Thank you for journeying to Wild Horse, Wyoming, with me.

As always, wishing you love and peace,

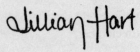

Questions for Discussion

1. What are your first impressions of Eloise? How would you describe her? What do you think she is looking for? What does she fear most when Sean spots her cane?

2. What are your first impressions of Sean? Are you surprised at his reaction to Eloise's disability? What does this tell you about his character? How do you know he's a good man?

3. What do you think of Eloise's grandmother? What role does she play in the story? What advice does she give Eloise? Have you ever had a family member like Gran?

4. What do you think of Sean's intention to be a lone wolf? What function does this serve for him? How does he use the excuse to keep his heart safe?

5. How did Eloise's accident affect her? How have all the losses that followed affected her?

6. Family, friends and the town speculate about Eloise and Sean's relationship. What part do they play in the budding romance? How does this affect Eloise? Sean?

7. Why does Eloise reject Sean's kiss? How does this affect her? Affect Sean?

8. What are Sean's strengths as a character? What are his weaknesses? What do you come to admire about him?

9. What values do you think are important in this book?

10. Little Julianna Stone wants every homeless animal to be saved and to find a home. What Biblical basis is there for her wish? What impact does Julianna's hope have on the story? On Eloise and Sean's romance? What impact does one little girl make?

11. What do you think are the central themes in this book? How do they develop? What meanings do you find in them?

12. In the beginning of the story, Eloise wrestles with the losses resulting from her car accident. What does she learn by the end of the story? How has God given her more than the accident took away?

13. How does God guide both Eloise and Sean? How is this evident? How does God gently and quietly lead them to true love?

14. What role do the animals play in the story? Have you ever helped an animal in need?

15. There are many different kinds of love in this book. What are they? What does Eloise learn about true love?

INSPIRATIONAL

Inspirational romances to warm your heart & soul.

TITLES AVAILABLE NEXT MONTH

Available August 30, 2011

HER RODEO COWBOY
Mule Hollow Homecoming
Debra Clopton

THE DOCTOR'S FAMILY
Rocky Mountain Heirs
Lenora Worth

THE RANCHER'S RETURN
Home to Hartley Creek
Carolyne Aarsen

A FAMILY OF THEIR OWN
Dreams Come True
Gail Gaymer Martin

SAFE IN HIS ARMS
Dana Corbit

MENDED HEARTS
Men of Allegany County
Ruth Logan Herne

LICNM0811

REQUEST YOUR FREE BOOKS!

2 FREE INSPIRATIONAL NOVELS
PLUS 2
FREE
MYSTERY GIFTS

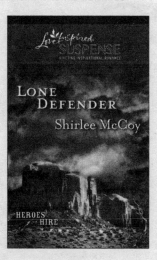

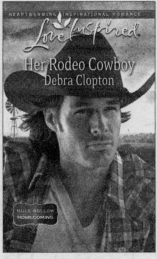